# THE ROAD TO GULANSHARO

## Book Two of The Knight in the Panther Skin Trilogy

*An accurate English prose adaptation of Shota Rustaveli's epic 12th century Georgian poem.*

H. J. BUELL

ANA GABUNIA

https://hjbuell.com

# COPYRIGHT AND PRINTING

ISBN-13: 978-1-7379516-3-6 – eBook
ISBN-13: 978-1-7379516-5-0 – Paperback
ISBN-13: 978-1-7379516-7-4 – Hardcover

First Printing, July 07, 2022

Happy Birthday to Henry, Sam, and David!
I love you more than salt.
♥

# ACKNOWLEDGEMENTS

## ARTWORK
Irakli Kakhadze, Cover Artwork
Dasha Vainstein, Layout and Design

## CONTENT EDITORS
Michael Arizola, Tyron Eugene Byrd Jr.,
Dane Muckler, Ph.D., Abbi Seid

## DEVELOPMENTAL EDITORS
Zobaid Alam, Luka Bandzeladze,
Lucie Isabelle Sylvaine Dubail, Arkadius Dziminski,
Diana Kakhidze, Benjamin Kastin, Robin Kershaw,
Alexander Edward Loughead, Loïg Seigneur,
Marek Suliga, Khatia Turmanidze,,
Victor-Hugo Vaca II, Nina Vaxanski, Edward Wilson

## MUSIC AND AUDIOBOOK
David (Dato) Toradze – https://toradze.ge

## SPECIAL ACKNOWLEDGEMENTS
Darina, Veronica, Angelina & Max,
Desert Knights of America MC, AS from Reddit,
Josiah Keola Blair, Julie Cheung, Ali Farhad Howaida,
David Jakobia, Rishi Lakhani, John Jeys, Virgil Jones III,
Tina Mamulashvili, Patrick Naughter, Lasha Pataraia,
The Rat, Sea Dog, Rezo Tchelidze, Tom Vainstein,
Marjorie Wardrop, and Chef Gustavo from
https://www.blankslateband.com

# SOMETIMES I REMEMBER YOU IN A SONG

### H. J. Buell

*Sometimes it's spring. It's green everywhere I look. I'm sitting in the middle of a field with you. We just met, but it feels like forever. The grass is wet. We're wet. Everything is wet.*

*It's raining, and we're dancing under the stars. Your eyes shine like summer. You smile as the water runs down your face. It kisses the corners of your mouth, and I want to drink you like wine.*

*Today the air is crisp. You compare it to an apple. Leaves. Every color everywhere. Each one bright as your laugh. Autumn seems such a sad name for something so beautiful. Someone.*

*You promise, but promises are for winter. It's cold. We can't remember the words, except, maybe I do. Is it snowing? Everything is white, but all I can see are your footsteps.*

*Your toes curl around my finger. It's my favorite thing for a day. I want to never leave this moment. But we can't hold it all, and I don't know the season. Still, I hold your hand.*

*Dreams that don't fly are never free. They take root and become prisons to our hearts, but you ask if hope still nests in their branches. I don't know. I'm afraid to look. My steps seem small again.*

*Everything fades into the fog. It's beautiful, though I miss you by my side, I might not know you anymore, but some moments never fade. Sometimes I remember you in a song.*

# PREFACE

The Road to Gulansharo is a bridge between two parts of an adventure few people outside of Georgia have ever heard of. It's about what people are capable of when they aren't afraid to be honest with themselves. More, this book is a faithful adaptation of the original Knight in the Panther Skin, composed by Shota Rustaveli in 12th century Georgia.

Although little is known about Shota, the poem's prologue indicates it was written to praise the first female ruler of Georgia - Tamar Mepe (King Tamar). Some believe Shota was in love with her, as his writings allude to this. But, like all great works, the original is not without controversy or debate.

To this day, his writing is a pillar of Georgian culture. It stands alone as the most significant literary accomplishment of Georgia. The original poem is written in Rustavelian Quatrains, consisting of four sixteen syllable rhyming lines. In total, the poem comprises 1,662 of these, totaling 6,648 lines. Each year in Georgia, there are people who recite the entirety of these verses from memory at annual events.

We've done our best to accurately capture the spirit and meaning of the story. However, cultural, and linguistic barriers limit the ability of anyone to fully express the true beauty of this text in anything other than its original Georgian form. However, what you read in this book is the most honest and accurate adaptation of Shota's poem as an English literary novel.

For additional resources, comments, and information about the country and traditions, please visit our website.

## https://hjbuell.com

# TABLE OF CONTENTS

# INTRODUCTION –

## REDISCOVERING THE MAGIC

When my journey began, I met an impossible man in a time and place where he shouldn't have existed. Of course, it wasn't my first time encountering the unexpected, but meeting him was different than anything I'd ever experienced. He gave me a story before vanishing, or at least part of the tale. The poetry of what he shared was a priceless gift to me. A kiss from a foreign place that left hints of familiarity in its passing.

However, as drinking sometimes did, my wine from the night before left my head feeling like it was where my feet should have been. But a bright Georgian sun beckoned from my window, as did the delightful scents of home-cooked food wafting up the stairs. I can't say I remember how I made my way home from the wine bar to my hostel, but, like all wild things, I did know where to find breakfast.

Once I'd satisfied my hunger, I began reviewing the

1

notes in my journal. With more than a bit of help from my hosts, I booked a trip to Tbilisi. They told me the city was the capital of modern Georgia, but the word 'modern' left me wondering what older cities might have once been more important. But I didn't have time to discuss this. The driver was waiting, and I needed to collect my things.

As I packed my bags and left the hostel, I wondered at the shifts in countries and cultures I'd seen as I traveled from place to place. Everywhere I went, cities and people were different as the dialects of their citizens, and all of them seemed in a race to become something they weren't and never had been. Yet, culture and tradition remained strong in some places. I hoped this would be one of them. Almost everywhere else seemed intent on bartering away their unique identities in exchange for western fantasies.

Coming from America, it always pained me to watch people exchange history for modernization and material possessions. I recognized the modern American dream for what it was. A beacon, glowing and shining like the mirage of lies which sustained Las Vegas. Everything about it was a fantasy. However, like pilgrims lost in the desert and stumbling towards a mirage, too few people considered the cost of attaining that dream.

Give us your culture and history, the lie promised, and you can do anything. Sleep, they said, and the world will be new when you wake. Yet far too many people overslept in the mists of this fantasy. They forgot their roots by the time they woke and ended up wasting all they could have been. This was truth behind the lie they dreamt. But no one recognized this until it was too late.

These were the things I thought of as I made my way to Tbilisi. We drove past small towns and villages. Meanwhile my guide spoke of America and Russia in the same breath. Complaining about the sorrow these nations left in their wake. He called them imperialist empires, asking why the leaders of capitalist and communist governments were so unconcerned about the damage they caused. But I had no answer for him. I was only a writer and did not yet know the things I have learned since.

I listened with curiosity as we crossed over mountains and through lush green fields. Much of what he said had a ring of truth, but I didn't want his opinions to color my impressions of Tbilisi. However, as we neared, I was surprised to see the reality of what he said.

Skeletons of Soviet style housing tenements poked their way through the distant skyline. All I could think of when I saw it was what he told me of imperialism continuing to smile false promises from the ashes of communism. Those buildings reminded me of rotten teeth hanging from the mouth of an old beggar.

Once we got close to the city, the buildings changed. New high-rise apartments began to take shape, creeping into the sky like beacons of foreign influence. They broke the monotony of decay ringing the city. At least, until we reached the center.

There, to my surprise, I saw a hideous towering black monolith looming over classical architecture and historic cobbled streets. The shadow it cast reminded me of Tolkien's overlord Sauron, wilting the roses beneath it. Yet there was also so much history everywhere I looked. Perhaps I could find what I was looking for down an old avenue.

I took a room overlooking a place called Freedom Square. At first glance, it was fascinating. The circle was lovely, and a gold capped monument of Saint George slaying a dragon crowned the pillar in the middle.

However, once I'd settled in, I was surprised and to find gaudy and overpriced shops. Burberry, and Cartier were squeezed between panhandlers jostling for sales and grasping at coins from tourists. Disappointed, I left the main streets for less touristy haunts. But with every step, I felt the decay of something magnificent.

Bits of history were tucked away on back streets, far from the modern facades sold to visitors from abroad. Few of the people around me paid attention to the crumbling cobblestone alleys and broken stairwells. Yet, I couldn't stop myself from seeing them. They beckoned me to remember an old city people were forgetting with each new building. It was as if the streets pleaded with me to wake up from the dream and see the cancer consuming this once-majestic city.

I found sellers of every kind in every place I went. In the tunnels, street musicians sang their renditions of Adele and Billie Eilish. Meanwhile, beggars littered the entrances of metro stations like discarded McDonald's cups. Each of them was a testament to the sale of culture and independence. And for what? All I saw for sale was the unrealized and largely failed hope of a western dream.

For several days I searched the capital, looking for another thread to the tale of Shota Rustaveli. But I found nothing to bring me back to the magic of the story. I collected countless clues in the museums and from statues throughout the city, yet never what I was seeking. Everything there was too dry for me to swallow. It was all packaged for tourists, but I was an artist.

One day I was sipping coffee in an old café while listening to a woman read stories and legends from Georgian history. She spun tales of forgotten myths and legends coming to life in the architecture of old places. One tale in particular caught my attention.

She told of how Georgian heroes fought to defend Bagrati Cathedral from the Ottoman Empire. Then she said the sounds of those men and women fighting for country and life could sometimes still be heard on certain nights of the year. The woman went on with tales of magic in what she called the White City of Kutaisi. The cradle of Georgian culture and oldest city in the country. Like a moth to a flame, her stories drew me in. Before long I was on a minibus called a marshrutka, and on my way to see the legends and places she spoke of.

The trip was largely uneventful, and before long, I had rooms in an old building at the center of town. Though I hadn't seen much of Kutaisi yet, the few people I met in the streets spoke volumes with their behavior. Everyone was polite, and for a moment I imagined myself back in Kvareli. Looking around I realized this was where I needed to be.

I had entered a city from another age. Old buildings were restored to their former grandeur or in the process of being revitalized. People carried themselves with pride and had a different character than what I encountered in Tbilisi. As I walked, I found cafes and art galleries, with tiny bits of the west tucked here and there between antique shops and phone repair booths.

My little jaunt took me past an enormous square overflowing with old books. Forgotten authors, broken spines, and missing covers almost spilled out into the streets. The place was beautiful in a way like nowhere else I had been. Everything was different, including the beggars. In fact, one offered to sell me an undoubtedly free flier for a performance.

I knew he was selling smoke, but his antics and animated dance pantomimes made the experience one I won't soon forget. Pretending to believe him, I argued his price down from paper money to a few coins. Fair payment for his efforts, though probably far too much to have paid. But it was worth it.

What I bought turned out to be an announcement for a classical dance performance honoring Shota Rustaveli's poem. It discussed the further travels of Avtandil, which

I was desperate to discover more about.

Moreover, the woman leading the dance was a study in elegance. Her name was Nino Ramishvili, and her image on the page seemed to come to life and speak to me. I could almost feel her reaching out across time, like Jane Seymour asking me to return to something I didn't know I had forgotten. The lure of a local dance about the story I chased was more than I could resist. At the appointed time, I went to the address and found an amazing old theater.

After handing my ticket over, I walked into an elegant piece of history straight out of the old world. The architecture and decorations were breathtakingly beautiful, and I wondered at the artisans who had built the place. Everyone around me also appeared to be from another time. But I didn't have the leisure to observe them. The lights were going down, and I needed to find my seat. Our show was about to begin.

The stage lit up, and the audience fell silent. My heart stopped when the curtain opened. The woman who came out had more grace and poise than anyone I had ever seen. With the first lift of her feet, my world shifted, and I was caught in the dance. Every step she took whispered hidden truths about the heroes I so desperately wished to learn more of.

I knew Avtandil had left the cave, but now I was going with him. Nino's dance carried me to a place I never dreamed of seeing. Before my eyes, the earth fell away. Soon I was riding with a lone Arabian man as he crossed the world towards impossible ends...

# CHAPTER 01 –

## ONE NIGHT CLOSER TO HOME

Many are the journeys a man takes in life. His steps forever lead from one event to another. Some paths yield fair results, while others end in tragedy. Though Avtandil once despaired of the road on which he discovered Asmath and Tariel, his spirits soared now. He was victorious in the face of certain defeat and returned home triumphant.

The life and dreams he once thought lost were renewed with each passing day. Every step was an elixir to his tattered soul, restoring strength and resolve. Though he had a month of untracked land before him, the sun and stars would show him the way.

He rode with a banner of love for Tinatin flying from his heart like the flag of victorious King. She, who he loved more than life. The news he carried was of success in his quest and the discovery of newfound friends. Though there was still much he needed to do, his first duty was to her. She would be the sole authority to measure his accomplishments.

As he traveled, his thoughts turned to the roads behind him, and the long years spent on them. Remembering the despair and emptiness which nearly consumed his soul, he wondered how much longer he could have gone on alone. At the same time, he marveled at the strength of Tariel, the Knight in the Panther Skin.

This was the man Avtandil had been in quest of for so many years. Yet, hurt had tarnished the heart of Tariel by the time the two men met. His was a closed fist of anger and bitterness towards the world of men, but somehow, he still clung to hope.

Where Avtandil often feared his own steps might falter, somehow, Tariel carried on. Chance encounters always managed to lift the dark and morose Knight over the death he begged for. This left the Arabian wondering. Had God's hand brought the two friends together?

Night after night, Avtandil found himself asking more profound questions about God and the meanings of life. As the days passed into weeks, he'd begun considering each of his actions over the last years. In particular, he thought of Tariel, who saw everything other than the face of God. Yet, turning away from the Creator had also turned him away from Nestan, the woman he loved and desired above all else. But she was lost. Perhaps forever.

Avtandil was different, though. For him, each step brought him closer to Arabia and the woman he longed to see more than the sun. He had never forsaken God. Nor had he abandoned his quest. But his thoughts did not soothe the lingering hurt he felt for those he left behind in the caves of the Devi.

# CHAPTER 02 –

## THE FORTRESS OF ARABIA

The pain of leaving his friends caused sorrow to darken him. It was as if each bit of joy in the steps he took was followed by an assassin, waiting to slay his happiness from the shadows. Sometimes he felt such deep and unrelenting loss at the absence of his newfound brother and sister that he scratched at his face and rent the rose of his cheeks. If it were it not for the joy of his imminent return to Tinatin, he feared the sadness of departing Tariel and Asmath might have ruined him.

It was as though his hands were left shorter and his reach less for want of those he had come to know and call his own. He worried the beasts of the wild might lick the blood dripping from the wounds his heart gave him. Yet, at the same time, his thoughts gave him greater cause to move more swiftly over the long road back to his home in Arabia.

A smile crossed his face when came to the desolate and

barren places where he first left the shelter of his youth. In the distance, he saw the imposing and impenetrable fortresses of the Arabian frontier rising from the earth. He was almost there. As he rode toward the walls, the men of the watchtower recognized him and cheered. He was their leader, and their devotion was unshakable. Their whole lives had been spent with him leading them in the defense of Arabia.

They quickly opened the gates, overjoyed to see him returned home safely. As the massive portcullis was lifted, and the ironwood doors opened, joyous men poured forth from the gates. They shouted to one another in happiness.

"He has returned! Our leader and brother is home! He who our days have been bitter from the loss of. Let us celebrate one and all."

From their midst, one caused the crowds to part. This was Shermadin, a lifelong friend and brother to Avtandil. They embraced with an intensity only strengthened by their years apart, and Shermadin cried out with happiness.

"How is it the destroyer of our enemy stands before me? Every day for nearly three years, I have sat on these walls in sorrow. Without solace, I have lit candles each night in the memory of your absence. My only hope has been looking towards the time of your return."

"Yet now I enjoy the reward of so much time spent on these battlements. From here, I watched every sunrise with little more than hope I might rest my eyes on you that day. And here you stand. My brother and my companion, words escape me."

"In the whole world, there is nothing to equal the joy in my heart from seeing you. I almost can't believe a mirage does not stand before me. How am I worthy of this moment, to welcome you safely back to the embrace of Arabia?"

As he spoke, the Knights around them bowed and

saluted. To a man, they held raised fists to their chests, overjoyed at seeing their General. Then Shermadin thanked God no grief afflicted their leader. One after another, every man came forward.

Their count was in the thousands, and all gave homage to Avtandil. Lords, leaders, and generals kissed his hands and feet. There was much jubilation, as everyone rejoiced at the return of their Hero.

Within the walls, there was a place the men had erected to feast when Avtandil returned. Now he stood before them, and they would celebrate. A more proud and merry assemblage of men had never been seen on any frontier. They gave him their highest respects, singing, and cheering for the man they had so deeply missed.

Shermadin sat closest to Avtandil, as is the way with brothers. Throughout the evening, the hero shared all that happened to him and everything he had seen. He finished with stories of Tariel, the Knight in the Panther Skin, who had won his heart. With tears and half-closed eyes, he said that without the Knight, it did not matter if he lived in a palace or a hut. All dwellings were the same without his other brother to share the comfort and joy.

In time, and with soft words, Shermadin explained to Avtandil all the news from the three years since his departure. None outside the walls knew he had left, for not even a whisper was raised of his absence. The drills and training of the soldiers had continued while he was gone, and the Kingdom was secure.

At once relieved and reassured by this news, Avtandil relaxed for the first time in in years. He feasted all night with his men, and when the sun kissed the sky, he departed. Tinatin waited for him, and he would not be delayed. As he made his way towards the palace, where he would meet Rostevan and his love, the frontier fortress of Arabia disappeared into the distance behind him.

# CHAPTER 03 -

## DAYS LONG DARKENED

Though he was full of joy at the promise of meeting friends he been long absent from, his heart was not whole. It bled with every step he took. In the absence of Tinatin, darkness sat over him like a brooding cloud. He missed her and desired nothing more than to gaze into her onyx eyes. To him, she was the rival of the sun.

Shermadin knew how Avtandil felt, and like any good friend, he came with the Hero and helped to carry the burden of his brother. Fast riders had been sent ahead of them to inform the King that Shermadin came with a message. But they were instructed not to share news of Avtandil's arrival. Instead, the hero would wait behind Shermadin so he could personally tell the King and his daughter, Tinatin.

His messenger arrived a few hours ahead of them, telling of good news from the far edges of the frontier. He said Shermadin prayed for an audience with King

Rostevan. Curious as to what the message might be, he prepared himself and waited in the audience hall. When at last Shermadin arrived, he came directly to the King, still dusty from the road, and begged leave to speak.

"My Lord, proud and mighty as you are, it is with equal measures of fear and precaution I come before you now. What I must say is not fully mine to share, though I can tell you this much."

"When none were able to find The Knight in the Panther Skin, and Avtandil saw your sorrow, he felt worthless at his failure. A burden dragged down his heart until he could no longer carry the weight of it. These past three years, he has been far from Arabia. He crossed the world and endured untold hardships to find this mysterious Knight. Now he has returned with news of him. He comes tonight in joy and safety and will tell you all on his arrival."

Rostevan stood in shock and surprise when he heard the truth of what had transpired over the last years. He was overjoyed at the prospect of seeing the youth he had so long missed. Now he knew why his foster son Avtandil had been absent so long. He smiled at the cunning of the clever youth, and the devotion his actions showed.

"The message you carry holds the world for me, for I have wished to see my son many times over these long years. This news brings deep joy to my heart. It is an answer to my prayers. Each day I asked God to return him safely from the frontier. So, it is a welcome thing to learn I will soon lay eyes on my son again."

Having spoken, the King gave Shermadin leave to rest and refresh himself. Yet, the man did not attend to himself. Instead, he went to Tinatin, a light the night was unable to darken. He asked to speak with her, and she invited him into her audience chamber, curious as to what he might have to say.

"My lady, I come to you on behalf of he whose absence has long darkened your days. He is coming to you this evening. What news he brings will please and brighten your days, which have no doubt been long in his absence."

Tinatin's heart leaped with joy and hope at the thought she would soon see the man she loved. Light flashed from her eyes, causing them to shine brighter than the sun. She gave him a gift, thanking him profusely. Though her father would meet the young Knight first, it did not diminish her joy in hearing she would soon see the man she loved.

She would be patient as a nightingale, as if she did not know her hero was coming. Her years had been spent waiting for him, and soon he would soothe the poison and ache which had so long debilitated her heart. All she had to do was wait.

# CHAPTER 04 –

## THE KNIGHT'S TALE

Rostevan soon grew impatient at the thought of waiting for Avtandil in the throne room. Gathering his guards, he rode out to meet the Knight. When the youth came into view, the two met like twin stars. Father and foster son embraced, and their hearts were overflowing with happiness. Around them, the many Lords and Ladies were so joyous they appeared drunk.

The King kissed the young Knight, and they hugged each other once more before mounting their steeds and riding toward the palace. Between them, the days of three years could almost be counted by their many smiles. Glad of heart, they entered the royal hall leaving their horses and men behind.

Tinatin, unable to keep herself away, was waiting inside. When she saw the hero, her crystal face beamed with a smile of tenderness towards him. The light from her eyes shone brighter than the Heavens. Nowhere on earth could have properly contained her happiness. The hero of Arabia had come home, a lion among lions. He bowed deeply when he noticed her, and her father smiled on the two of them.

A celebration was held that night, with an abundance of food and drink. All who came feasted on the bounty of the Kingdom. Rostevan and the young Knight talked throughout the evening. Their separation had torn the hearts of each, but it had not dimmed the light of their devotion.

Each of them enhanced the beauty and allure of the other, appearing to onlookers like the whisper of fresh snow or drops of dew beading on the petals of a rose. They gave gifts to those who had come. Small gold coins and pearls flowed like rivulets of water from a spring rain, running down the leaves of outstretched arms and into the hands of joyous people.

In time, those who celebrated the return of their hero had their fill of companionship and feasting. They left the halls, singing as they went, and departed for their homes. Only Sograt the Wise remained behind.

This was the Chief Advisor to the King, who guided him to crown Tinatin as Regent. Throughout Arabia he was known as the wisest person in the land. He waited for Avtandil with his advisors and a handful of the most important Lords. When the Hero came, they sat him before them. Rostevan asked about his journeys and what happened on the long road away from the Kingdom.

With a steady and strong voice, the Knight began his tale, asking not to be interrupted until he was done.

"I must beg your forgiveness if emotion overcomes me when I tell this story. What I say now pains my heart as if the tragedy were my own. The Knight in the Panther Skin is a man named Tariel. While he is human, there is little I can compare him to save perhaps the sun. His face is like light from the giver of life.

At once, it blinds and extinguishes the minds of all who

see him. Yet, for all his greatness, he has become like a wilted rose strangled by the thorns of Fate. It hurts me to tell you these things, for he who I speak of is far away and suffers an unbearable agony, yet I am not with him."

"When faith in another causes a man as much grief as he endures, the reed of his soul grows thin and brittle. The crystal of his face turns saffron. Though you only know and remember him as the one who sent so many of our Knights to an early grave, he is no monster. Rather, he bears pain and grief the deepest of seas cannot fathom."

"He is the last Prince and Lord of India. Across the vast expanse of their Seven Kingdoms, no one can equal or come close to him in battle. This much we saw in the fields when he slaughtered our soldiers. Yet, there is more to him. He has been separated from both his love and his Lordship. For nearly ten years, he has wandered, first with companions, and in the end alone, save one."

"The one who remains with him, his only comfort, is a woman named Asmath. Duty binds her to him more tightly than any Knight has ever served a King. It was she who bore witness to the beginning of India's fall, though it is a terrible story."

"Tariel was in love with the Princess of India, Nestan Daredjan, daughter of King Pharsidan and ruler of the Seven Kingdoms. But she was abducted by brutish Kadj sorcerers. Because of this and her devotion to Nestan, Asmath has followed Tariel across the world as he tries to rescue his beloved. Together, they have endlessly sought to find and free the woman they love from her captors."

"Unfortunately, duty forces me to relate the deeper tragedy of his story. They have utterly failed. However far and long each of them has searched, no one has been able to find Nestan or learn any news of where she is."

# CHAPTER 05 –

## A GHOST OF THE PAST

"After nearly three years of searching every corner of every place I went, I learned he was broken. No man can remain whole when he has lost so much and failed to achieve his goal. Despite this, he welcomed me and shared his tale. From there, we became closer than brothers born to the same mother. Our tragedies became as one."

"I learned the place he dwells was once a cave of the Devi, those other worldly creatures of old. They hollowed out halls and rooms from the rock with their unearthly and arcane abilities. But he and those he traveled with did not know the passages were home to monsters, or perhaps they would have fared differently."

"When they entered the caves, unseen enemies assaulted them from the shadows. The two Knights with him were unprepared for ferocity of the attack and could not defend themselves properly. They were slain by the foul magic of those three Devis. Yet Tariel managed to kill the creatures. However, he and Asmath were left alone. Now she is his only companion. It is her who comforts him and eases his suffering."

"Of Nestan, he has nothing other than the armlet she gave him. He wears the skin of a panther because it reminds him of her but refuses to wear the fine clothes and adornments of a Prince. Instead, he has chosen the company of beasts over men."

"The world is hidden to his eyes, lost in the shadows of smoke and ash blanketing the ruin of his life. He is consumed by the fires of agony. Their flames are endlessly renewed by the suffering each new dawn brings."

When Avtandil finished the story, his sorrow over the plight of his friend was clear to all. His only salvation was the sight of Tinatin, who smiled comfortingly whenever he looked at her. This caused rays of light to shine down, soothing his wounds like the sight of a sun through clouds over a field of new tulips.

The wise men and Lords of the Kingdom praised the strength he had shown in completing such a difficult quest. All were surprised and impressed by his ability to maintain such a difficult course. More than any other there, Rostevan was thankful for what his foster son had done.

Though the King had long since put the matter of the Knight in the Panther Skin away from his heart, his concerns over the stranger had never entirely left his mind. Were it not for the hero of Arabia, they might have stirred again one day. Yet, the actions of Avtandil had finally laid the King's hidden grief to rest.

Among all those gathered, none were happier than Tinatin. Though she was sad to hear the tragedy of Tariel and Nestan Daredjan, she could not help but rejoice at the return of her hero. The news he brought freed her from the shroud of grief gripping her for nearly four years, and she shone with pleasure like the light of the moon on new snow.

The rooms fell silent as the wise men and Lords finished discussing the Seven Kingdoms of India and Tariel. Soon they began to leave, returning to their homes or personal affairs. After everyone else left, the King and Tinatin bid goodnight to Avtandil and Shermadin. However, the two Knights remained, discussing events in Arabia until the hour grew late. Then they too retired to their chambers.

Avtandil had his servants ready a bath, and for the first time in years, he soaked the ache and dirt of the road from his weary bones. When clean, he changed into comfortable robes and sat next to the harp he had so often missed during his quest. He was playing a sad and mournful song to echo the longing in his soul when a ghost of the past came to his door.

A soft knock interrupted his repose, and like so many years before, he stood to answer it. Yet, this time, he was not surprised to see a servant of Tinatin. He expected she would secretly invite him to her rooms to speak in private, and it would be the first time he had been alone with her in three years. His joy could not be fully expressed. Though, he wondered what she might say after so many years apart.

# CHAPTER 06 –

## THE ROSE OF HIS SOUL

He traveled the empty corridors and hallways of the palace, as he had done when they last met. As he came to the door of Tinatin's apartments, he paused, composing himself before the servant opened the door and parted the curtain. Avtandil smiled when Tinatin called to him from within.

Stepping inside, he met the woman who held the desire and longing of his heart. This man, broken and whole in the same breath, had roamed the fields with lions until he became a lion. Yet he was still weary from the long road. He went to her, and the sight of her eyes removed the dull color from his demeanor, lighting his face like a new rose at dawn's first light.

She did not hide her admiration for the man before her. He had grown and changed, but her love was no less deep. When he left, he was only a man. But now, a Knight of the world stood before her. He was a priceless ruby, without equal, though still somewhat colorless. Separation from her appeared to have faded the red of his rose to a soft white.

Though he was unsure how she would welcome him after so long, a smile graced his face. His eyes shone like two brilliant diamonds as he gazed at her. For her part, she rested on a small velvet covered throne, majestic and unrestrained like the sun shining across an open sky of blue. Of all the fairest things planted in the garden of Eden, she was undoubtedly the most magnificent.

Her jet-black hair and eyebrows were bedecked with crystal and priceless gems. She was a woman watered by the generous hand of the Euphrates and grown like the sacred trees of Gabon. The form and curve of her body mirrored the Heavens. Among the language of ordinary men, no words existed to give sufficient praise to her. Over the whole earth, perhaps only the myriad tongues of Athenian sages could begin to describe her majesty and grace.

An empty chair rested before her, where she beckoned the joyful Knight to sit. He took his place, composing himself like a marble statue shaped from the unpolished whispers of the affection they shared. As they looked at one another, the emptiness of their years apart began to mingle with their longing.

Their mix of sweet and shy soon melted and mixed like honey into a hot cup of tea, until two things became one, and Tinatin began asking short and simple questions. Yet the cadence of her speech compelled a depth of emotion which added to the words she spoke.

"Today you told us of the one you sought. This Knight in the Panther Skin. The man named Tariel. Yet, as you spoke, I understood you would say more. As if the sun of your speech stood behind clouds. Though I know not whether the words you kept for yourself hold rain or skies of azure. What is it you wished to say yet did not share with my father?"

He paused, looking up from his hands and into the eyes of the woman he loved more than the world. For a moment, he stared into their inky black depths. They were deep pools in which he imagined no half-truth would be able to survive.

The thoughts which weighed on his heart were heavy. He was afraid they might drag her back into the darkness his quest had only just rescued her from. But in the end, he shared his burden with her.

"When a man carries desire in his heart, it holds him through time and space. Now, you ask me to recall the grief of days past. I feel it is unwelcomed to remember my sorrow, though I know no other way than to share it with you."

"The days which separated me from you have been long. Often, I feared they would never end. I crossed many mountains and rivers with nothing more than your name on my lips. The memory of our time together carried me through the most desolate of these places."

"Yet, in these spaces, despite the darkness of my time away from you, I found what we sought. The man was like a tree. Tall and unburdened by the weight of the world at first appearance. I thought it seemed as though the water of life gave him sustenance, and in him, I found a face carved like a rose. Yet I see now how vain my first perceptions were."

"The man I came to know was exhausted from the trials of his years. Though he wields a power like no other I have met, he was unable to withstand the turning of the earth. Despite this, he spoke to me as a brother and an equal."

"We were one, with no bridges between us. He was the sun, and I the moon. Truly, it breaks my heart to relate this to you. However, it is my sworn duty to both you and him that I should share the story."

"I can speak no praise of him which you would understand from my words alone. For those few who have seen him, there is nothing else to give pleasure. The eyes of all who rest on his form are weakened as if staring into the sun's brilliance. But the world and life have become no more than beasts for him. He runs alone, lost in his grief and weeping in the fields."

"The rose of his soul has turned saffron in color. But the violence of his spirit gathers like a noose around his neck. He has become one with the panther whose skin he wears. Trails wind down from the caves he calls home. Yet, I do not know which of those paths he takes when he leaves, or where he goes from there."

"A lone damsel is his only companion. She remains in the cave when he goes out, chained to him by the devotion of her heart. It is she who holds him and bears his sorrow. In doing so, she maintains his life. But it pains me to recount this."

"He is no different than you or me. No more, or less, but somehow separated and lost to all we are still able to love and cherish. This is in part why I came to love him, for it is our faith and devotion to life which makes us shed tears for the pain others find themselves in."

# CHAPTER 07 –

## More Than Salt

Avtandil paused for a moment, and then began telling of finding the Knight in the Panther Skin and following him across the plains for three days. He hung his head in shame at recounting his assault on Asmath. But he smiled when describing her wisdom and how they became brother and sister.

No detail was spared, and he carefully recounted each moment and word of the tale Tariel wove in the caves of the Devi. When he came to the end of his story, he told of leaving. He explained how Asmath went to the edge clearing when he left and begged a promise of his return before the first spring flowers faded.

When Tinatin heard the last words of his story, the well of her desire was filled. Her face shone like a full moon, and she spoke for the first time since he started telling his tale.

"That which was before a chain about my heart and

pained my every waking moment is now cut loose. Yet, I do not know what answer I can make which will give comfort to this broken Knight. How can we return the pleasure of life to him? What balm or salve can we use to heal his wounds and restore him to the world of men?"

Avtandil thought long before responding and, in the end, answered with slow and measured words.

"I have promised them I would return. It was sworn in your name, for there is no greater thing a man can swear by than the sun of his life. In doing so, my soul is torn. While I willingly sacrifice myself for his cause, I fear it may cost me you, who has no equal."

"I believe a friend should give his heart in exchange for the hearts of those he protects. Love is both a road and a bridge, so no trouble should be spared for the sake of aiding his friends. Though I love you and wish nothing more than to be by your side, I cannot help but think of his beloved."

"His grief for Nestan must be equal to mine were I to have lost you. Because of this, my own joy is no more than an empty cup if I do not find a way to help him. But no one other than me can do what needs to be done, and I do not know how to proceed."

"I'm not able to run off into the hills in a blind effort to save him, yet I refuse to allow him to be brought to ruin. He wished to die and told me as much. His prayers to God for an end to his suffering go unanswered. Now he waits for my return. With each moment I delay, the fire raging in his heart burns him further. But what person has confidence in a rash man? I should plan, but how?"

Tinatin gently placed her hand on Avtandil's head, and the sun-like one smiled and spoke to him.

"For all your prowess, you are still a man. In part, this is why I love you so much. You do not see how all my desires have been fulfilled. First, and most important to me, you have returned home safely. Second, you have found what was lost by discovering the Knight in the Panther Skin. And finally, the love seeded in my heart has grown these many years we've been apart. Your heroism has brought home a boon to soothe my aching heart. Before, I was burdened with chains. This was the reason for your quest, but now I am freed by your hand."

"I am sure your time in this world has taught you Fate treats every man like the weather. Some days our sun is bright and shines down upon golden fields of wheat. On others, it lights the sky with fire, and wrath thunders down from the heavens. Only yesterday, grief gripped my soul. However, joy and happiness have now fallen on me like a rain of apple blossoms. Seeing how brightly my world is lit with joy, I must ask myself, why should anyone else be sad?"

"I am happy to hear you would not break the oath you swore. The duty of men is to keep the truth of what they promise and fulfill their vows. More importantly, love amongst friends must always be honored. These things in your heart are the smallest part of my love for you. But they build the foundation of my respect in you as not only the man I love but as a man of the world."

"There is no question to me of what you must do. You need to seek a cure for this Knight and find a way to learn what is unknown. Your road must take you to those places he has been unable to discover. Neither of us has a choice in this matter, or all we hope to build together will rest on a lie, and I would not have our future built on the sands of betrayal."

I will accept your duty to him as a service to me. Therefore, you must return to those caves and aid your friend. It does not matter what it takes or how far you must go. I would not have a man beside me who betrayed his sworn brother and was a faithless oath breaker."

"The man I have chosen is you, as I am your chosen woman. Because of this, we each must sacrifice what we desire today. This is how to make the world better for our children and ourselves."

"But what am I to do while you are gone? When the sun and light of my life are hidden from me again, how will I keep myself from sorrow's grasp? Duty compels you to leave my side and fulfill your vows. It is my hand which compels you to go, however much you may wish to stay."

"As I have said, what you do for him is also a duty to me. I cannot allow you to forsake him or your promise. Yet I fear I must remain luckless. Bereft of your light, I fear to grow cold in the absence of your warm and strong embrace. Do not linger too long. When you are gone, I will miss you more than salt."

# CHAPTER 08 –

## MORNING COMES TOO SOON

Avtandil let out a long and drawn-out sigh when he heard her words. It was like the quiet breath of a singer beginning the chorus. When he answered, his words were laced with the pain of what he must do.

"I would perhaps make an ode to those who love, for where I carried seven woes before, my duty to you has united them into eight. It is vanity for one frozen to blow on the water for warmth. So, I will not seek comfort in what cannot be had. Yet love can also be vain, resting in the last kiss of a setting sun or a rising moon."

"The song of eternity is sung forever between those two celestial lovers who never unite. When I am next to you, I only carry this pain once. Yet if I leave, the hurt increases a thousand times."

"Open your window and you will see the new season approaching. When it ends, the dusty and fire-laden winds of the simoom will blow and burn all who wander.

For me, I think my lot in life is to be lost and burned. I am separated from all I love. What I want leaves me no choice other than to shoot my heart like a target. From today I fear my life is shortened by a third."

"Though I crave refuge from the storm, the time for seeking shelter against trouble has passed me. There are no ports to protect or shelter me from what I must do now. The time for seeking safety passed with my youth, and I feel the weight of love and the burden of duty on a man. There is no alternative course. I must venture into the unknown once more."

"You, my love, have spoken and I understand your commands. It pains me to discover the rose of peace I sought has so soon revealed its thorns. But it seems I should be perfect to reach what I desire most. For this reason, I must beg you to become a second sun for me. Let me carry a token of hope and life in my breast as I depart the comfort and home of my beloved Arabia. I would not weather this night anywhere other than with you."

The Knight spoke in soft and deep tones, and she looked up at him with more than curiosity in her eyes. He shared what was on his heart and mind, his words adding fuel to the fires growing between them. Soon their meeting grew more intimate than at any time in the past. The lights of desire left no shadows between them, and the first drop of nectar fell from the flower.

They caressed the lines and curves of their faces until each was infused with the ruby glow of passion. Like pearls grown from the sands of life, their innermost secrets shimmered and were reflected in the eyes of one another. Each shared breath pulled them closer together, perfecting and fulfilling their desire.

For, what better thing exists for a man and a woman than to approach one another in the garden of life? Together, hero and heroine found a moment removed from the pain of the world. In that space their chests rose and fell with the rhythm of the earth. Hands followed the sun's path until discovering the starlit parts of the moon. And every color from every season was shared between them until all colors became one.

They planted seed in the garden, for this was what they wanted. And from these moments, a tree would grow. All who have ever gazed on what love causes to blossom find joy. But those who never see it only hold sorrow, for they do not know what secrets the night holds.

Yet, duty and responsibility necessitated their parting. They could not stay together like this, and their removal from one another was not the bittersweet joy poets so often write about. Instead, it was a weal upon their souls. In their hearts, their separation the wellspring of sorrow. Yet neither told the other of this. He did not want her to suffer more, and she was afraid to erode the foundation of his resolve.

With one last embrace, they left one another. Avtandil held his head high as he went from her chambers. But when he reached the outer courtyard, his steps faltered. Severed from his love, he made his way home in the dark, stumbling along as though in a daze.

To him, the morning sun would soon shed tears of blood more abundant than the sea from which his hurt welled. As he walked, he aired but a single sentence of his grief aloud, hoping the heavens might hear the pain their idle hands caused him.

"Fate drinks my blood, and there is no end to her thirst."

# CHAPTER 09 –

## THE BARD'S TALE

Avtandil continued into the night, his heart burdened by an unceasing melancholy. It pulled him down into the depths of despair and he beat himself in the chest until leaving a bruise. But the hurt did not lessen the ache in his soul. He already knew love was fickle. She made men weep and melted their hearts, but the knowledge did nothing to ease his hurt. He was powerless to stop his feelings.

Life was like this. When clouds hide the sun, the earth is cast into shadow. For him, leaving his beloved was no different. All the world was lost to him in the twilight of separation. There would be no more mornings for him until he was with his love again.

Tears of frustration sprung from his eyes and made rivers down his cheeks as though cast in blood. He spoke aloud, lamenting the tortures Fate once more heaped upon him.

"I fear my beloved is not satisfied with me, for I have sacrificed myself to comfort my brother Tariel. The brand of her black eyelashes sears my heart. Though I may be made of adamant, there will be no light for me until I see her again. Joy and life now sit together in my hands, like dust in an empty and forgotten cup."

"Yesterday I returned home, tall, and strong as the youngest trees which have grown up in the garden of Eden. Today I am brought to nothing. I have caught myself in a net of fire that cannot be quenched or stopped. Fate endlessly thrusts through my soul with her lance. She cuts through me like a razor, leaving my spirit in tatters."

"All around me, I stare at what is left. Now more than ever I know the way of the world. All our lives are nothing more than a rambling bard's tale. A babble of nonsense like a brook through the forest, where none can find sustenance or peace."

Trembling and shuddering with the pain of these newfound revelations. He ground his teeth, but it did not lessen the agony of his predicament. Instead, it felt as though he chewed on shards of glass. He longed to talk to Tinatin again, for conversation and time spent with those loved are always preferable to their absence. But the time for talking was gone. Now he was compelled to action.

These were the lessons the bitterness of parting taught him. Left too long, the heart becomes tarnished and dull like a cup of silver. Through the deceit of Fate, what was once glorious and full of bright ends had become shrouded in swaths of darkness. His heart, he knew, would be no different. Time might dull his pain, but it would forever mark him.

With these thoughts weighing heavily on his mind, he made his way home. His couches beckoned like the sea to a ship, and he fell on them in a heap of sorrow. The agony of what he must do was beginning to wear through him.

His heart felt like the tattered ends of flag, forgotten, and left hanging over a defeated and abandoned fort.

No different than a wounded soldier returning to such a place after a fierce battle, he did not know how deeply he had been cut until the fight was finished. Now he could see the true extent of the damage he suffered.

Before, he had been sheltered in the light of his loved one. But now he was truly separated from her. He had no choice but to endure his burden. However, agony caused the glow from his face to fade like a rose bathed in darkness. The sun was indeed gone from his sight.

He laughed to himself as he thought of men and their folly. They are greedy and harbor an insatiable desire for joy above all else. Yet, in the end, the grief they must carry counts at a much greater cost than any happiness they attain. Their hearts are perverse and unable to justly measure these things.

Neither King nor death itself could master the wiles of such a thing. Nor could it overcome the walls a man must build to contain so much pain. These were the truths he spoke to his heart, but it appeared to be deaf. Instead, he might have tried holding a cup up to the rain, hoping to catch wine. Better still if he wore fine robes and tried to chase beggars from his side. In either case, he would enjoy more success than talking to himself had won him.

Now he, like Tariel, wore a token of his love. Tinatin had wrapped a golden string of pearls and rubies around his arm when he left. In his mind, they reminded him of her brilliant teeth and the lips which hid her smile. He would forever keep these tokens close to his heart. A reminder of what he longed to have and what pain he carried in not having it.

As a salve on his wounds, he forced himself to remember her beauty. He imagined kissing her mouth, from which grace itself was born. His joy at her memory flowed like the tears of the fabled river Pison, one of the four which watered Eden. Above all, he remembered the smile she gave him as they parted, falling asleep to the thought of her fingers slipping from his as he slipped into a dreamless sleep.

# CHAPTER 10 –

## THE HEART WHICH HUNTS

In the morning, Avtandil woke to the sound of a man at
the door. His sleep had been deep and undisturbed.
Despite the pain in his heart, he was refreshed. He stood
and went out to greet the man, who summoned him to the
King's court. Proud and gentle, he walked into the
brightness of dawn and mounted his horse.

He arrived to find a crowd of spectators packed so
tightly they were almost standing on top of one another.
They cheered at the sight of him. He turned and waved,
seeing Rostevan ready to take to the fields. Trumpets
sounded the march, and Avtandil gave himself up to the
chase he realized the King had planned.

Men of the hunt rode forward as one, moving in step to
the thunderous beat of copper drums. It was as if each man
had become the battering ram of a warship, surging
forward across a sea of sound. They would ride into their
quarry with the force of their march, battering and

breaking the beasts into submission. There was so much noise nothing anyone said could be heard. But it did not stop the hounds from chasing their game from the forests, while hawks flew in such numbers the sun was darkened.

All the lords and attendants of the King came with them. They rode out and descended on the fields like a cloud of locusts. Not a creature escaped them or the intensity of their hunt, and when they finished, the land was red with the blood of the animals they brought down.

They returned home to couches and pavilions, each adorned with decorations and lights to celebrate the Hero of Arabia returning home. The King sat and beckoned Avtandil to sit next to him, which he did without hesitation. Around them, a choir of singers softly caressed the mood of the evening, accompanied by harp and lute players. They extolled the bravery and glory of those who hunted and more, the deeds of Avtandil.

The two men spoke to one another. Though many a guest sat near them, none were close. They talked long and with an intensity unmatched by the other guests. The crystal and ruby of their cheeks flashing like lightning in the night. Some few leaned in to catch what the two said. But the noise of the crowds kept their words secret. Other than the name of Tariel, no one knew what they said.

When they finished feasting, it was late in the evening and much of the crowd had dispersed. Avtandil's words with his foster father were heavy on his mind. He realized no one else understood the burden Tariel carried. This knowledge hung like a stone about his neck, but he did not bow beneath its weight. At least he was not entirely alone, for Tinatin understood his pain and the sacrifices he needed to make.

But pain filled the basket of his heart, and he thought sorrow would forever be a companion. He wondered, with all he must do, how he might make a place for himself and the woman he loved. Once more, each step he took towards his house was hounded by thoughts of the duty hanging over him.

When he came home, he felt as if he stepped into the abode of a stranger. Like a lost man, he craved rest, but there was no chance for this. Instead, he paced back and forth. Sometimes he would lay down, and in the next minute, he would stand. His thoughts alternated between Tinatin and Tariel, and the gulf of uncertainty yawning before the way forward threatened to consume him.

Eventually, he tried to calm his mind and take refuge in sleep. Hoping his bruised heart would listen to his prayers for patience and wisdom, he spoke to himself. Perhaps the voice of his spirit would soothe the wounds on his soul.

"How I wish for respite from these trials, though it might make a grave of my heart to seek it. I dare not imagine what I must say to console the fires raging in me. My hands are empty, and I feel this will cause the desolation of all my hopes and dreams. Yet I still yearn to find a measure of peace or sustenance for my spirit."

"I stand on the farthest edge of a gorge. Tariel stands on the other side, tall and firm like a tree. I wish to be on the same ground as him, yet we are separated, and I need him. But only Tinatin understands what I feel. She knows how those who lay eyes on him find their hearts swooning with joy. Some cannot gaze into the light of his form, yet he and I are of equal measure. Perhaps if I slept, I might find him in a dream, but rest appears denied to me."

"Though I wish these for things, one man's hands can only contain so much. I know it is not now in my power to hold everything I desire. So, I must not waste myself grasping at what I am unable to reach. Instead, I need to remind myself patience is the fountainhead of wisdom."

"What if I am unable to withstand my pain? How can

I accomplish anything? I need to find a way to adapt myself to the anguish of life. If I would have happiness from God, I must also accept the grief so frequently laid upon me."

"In this knowledge, I will seek sanctuary. For I must not allow my pain to break me. Like a ship lost at sea and tossed from one wave to another, I will endure separation from those I love. However much my soul may wish for death over the suffering of life, I have no choice. If my heart belongs to others, I must sacrifice myself for them."

"Though, perhaps sharpest amongst the pains I bear is my love for Tinatin. It hurts me to continue hiding my feelings for her from everyone. Yet the flame and fire of our love must be seen by none, for it is unbefitting of me to expose the truth of her heart or mine."

The hero finally drifted off to sleep as the last words left his lips. For a time, his worry and hurt were held at bay. His weary soul took refuge in a dreamless void until the sun kissed the edges of the sky, and he was once more brought into the light.

# CHAPTER 11 –

## THE TRUTH BEHIND A SMILE

Avtandil woke and opened his eyes, blinking in the brightness of the morning sun. The radiant dawn lit the world around him, and the night had gone. He felt surprisingly refreshed and began planning his course for the day. As he dressed, he discussed his thoughts with himself.

"If I would not reveal my love, I must continue to keep it concealed. However, there are those who are wiser than I. Perhaps they may help me find the way forward. The best of them is Sograt, chief advisor to the King. He is wise above all others and knows the ways of the heart and the world. I need to seek out his advice."

Thinking this, he left his home and made his way to the wise man's home. Sograt had always been his friend and a tutor. More importantly, he was one of the most trusted men in the Kingdom. Perhaps, by the grace of God, the wisdom Avtandil sought might be found within the domain of Sograt's vast experience.

However, much to his dismay, Sograt was not home. Instead, the second wisest man in the Kingdom was there. He was the vizier Ustasra, and Avtandil had seen him at the King's council. He knew the man, though not well.

After a moment, the advisor came out to greet the Knight, paying homage and respect before speaking.

"I think the sun has risen upon my house this day. News of your many accomplishments is shared throughout the palace, and there is joy in your arrival. I have listened eagerly to stories of you. It is an honor to entertain you as my guest and offer my services."

Ustasra was the picture of eloquence, observing every formality and etiquette of Arabia. He came and helped Avtandil dismount and invited him into the house of Sograt. They rested on an old Cathayan rug, while servants brought sweet mint tea. The fragrance of incense was pleasantly thick in the air, and glass lanterns illuminated the house like beams of afternoon sunlight.

They spoke at length about nothing, while servants came and went, bringing fresh teas and small sweets to eat. Each respectfully addressed Avtandil, offering perfectly formed words of praise for him. But the Knight was not there for pleasantries.

He was a man seeking wisdom from a well, and the advisor, a study in patience, waiting like the water below. But this was the way of sages and wise men. They know a welcome guest should have a cheerful host. For when one is relaxed, only then can the truth be measured.

Because of this, the advisor was not idle. He saw to every comfort, knowing there was some other reason for this visit than tea and conversation. Yet, the day passed by with no meaningful discussion. Clearly, Avtandil was waiting for something.

Servants bustled around them, at times more numerous

than ants. Occasionally they could be heard whispering blessings to themselves with joy at the sight of their hero. It was as if a wind from the west brought them the fragrance of roses, and all were drunk from it.

The Knight sat opposite the advisor, resting on the comfortable Cathayan rug. Yet every time their speech drifted towards important matters, another servant appeared, swooning in the presence of Avtandil. Ustasra chased them away more than once, until the household was quiet and the two of them were left alone. They could finally enjoy the sanctity and peace of the room they sat in.

Avtandil, sipping his tea, took in the measure of the man before him. Though he had seen this advisor, he did not know him. Long ago, life taught him the most trustworthy men were not always the most intelligent. In fact, the closer one went to any city's heart, the less a man of words and learning could be trusted. Yet, Sograt was a lifelong friend. He was no fool, and this man was second to him. So, Avtandil addressed Ustasra and carefully asked his question.

"In the councils and chambers of the Lords, nothing is hidden from Sograt or his wisdom. I think you who sit next to him must share a similar mind. Though I must ask, where is he, most wise of our Kingdom's advisors?"

Ustasra turned to him and smiled. Thoughts unknown to the Knight were beneath the smile. Little did he know, it would not be long before he learned the truth behind the man's smile. But before Avtandil could consider the matter, the advisor spoke, revealing where Sograt had gone.

# CHAPTER 12 –

## DUTY TO THE KINGDOM

"The wisest of men in our Kingdom has left. He has gone far into the western realm of Greece. There, he seeks counsel concerning the one you spoke to the King of. This Indian named Tariel, the Knight in the Panther Skin."

"Sograt hopes to learn more of your tale in the city of Athens, for it is home to wisdom collected over thousands of years. Such events as you have spoken of in India will not have gone unnoticed by the wisemen there. They are of similar character and experience to our own Sograt."

"Unfortunately, it will be several months before he returns. As such, the duty of advising you falls to me. How is it I may help, and what might it be you seek of me?"

Avtandil thought for a moment on the words Ustasra spoke. With the chief advisor gone, he would need advice from another, but he did not want his plea shared with the entire council of wise men. This advisor was highly esteemed by Sograt. But could Avtandil trust him? He was not sure, but no other options were available. With nothing and everything to lose, he shared the truth of his heart with Ustasra.

"In the council chambers, nothing is hidden from the wise men. Your wisdom pierces every veil and ruse. The King does as you advise in matters of state and often agrees with your decisions. So, I must ask your advice. I beg you to listen to what I say. Perhaps your wisdom can cure me of this ailment I suffer. Offer me your guidance, so I might once again find myself as a whole man. Today I fear all that is left of my soul are tattered shreds of the hopes and dreams I once held."

"You spoke of Tariel earlier, so I understand you know the story of my travels. But I must tell you, the flames which consume him burn me in equal measure. I am slain with longing to aid his cause, though I do not know how to proceed. In being unable to accomplish what I desire, the well of my soul runs dry. You above all should understand how the love of a friend is a debt which cannot be ignored."

"My wisdom and patience remain with him. Yet there is nothing other than fire between our roads. I cannot reach him, who God created as a sun. For some reason, he has become my brother, and Asmath is now my sister. She means more to me than any sister by birth, for her faith in life caused me to accept her as my own."

"When I left them in the cave of the Devi, I swore an oath to return. I promised to come back before the first flowers of spring had faded, no matter the difficulty and burden of the road or how dark my heart might become. Knowing this, I have no choice but to make my way there. For what sort of man am I if I do not keep my vows?"

"This means I must leave Arabia, but the King has not

permitted me to go. These delays add fuel to these fires licking at my feet. However, I do not know how to get permission from Rostevan and still maintain my duties to the Kingdom."

"This is the truth of my heart. My words are not spoken as a braggart or one who wishes to inflate his worth. I cannot break my word and call myself a man in the same breath. Tariel and Asmath await me, yet I am unable to leave. It is not within me to abandon them, so I am driven mad by my predicament. For, when or where did anyone who breaks oaths ever prevail?"

"If you are willing, I must ask you to report these things to Rostevan. Explain how I feel and offer your wisdom to him regarding my plight. By my head, I swear, if he does not hold me here as a captive, I will not stay."

"Yet should he choose to make me his prisoner, what will he have from me? There will be nothing I can do except lament the pain and suffering of the brother I swore an oath to. So, I beg of you, help me. Do not let the fires of devotion destroy me."

"Let the King how I praise him from every mouth which can speak. Tell him I pray the light of God will assure him of my feelings towards him and respect for his wisdom and rulership. Yet, the Knight who awaits me is not one I can so easily put aside."

"Tariel is formed like a tree and has burned my soul with fire. Everything within me has been taken away by him. Even if I wanted to, there is no way I could keep myself from helping him. His tragedy is as sure as his honor. I can offer him no less in return."

"Please tell the King these words. 'Tariel holds my heart and honor. Without aiding him, I am useless to anyone. What will I do if I remain in the Kingdom? It is better for me to help my friend and brother. When I am done, I will return to my duties. Otherwise, I am lost.'"

"'In service to my friend, the glory of every victory will be yours, and yours alone. Yet should I fail to accomplish anything for him, I will rest my heart easily. My oath will not have been broken.'"

"'I beg you, do not let my departure grieve your heart or anger you. Whatever befalls me is the will of God. I pray He will grant you the victory I seek and send me, your ever-faithful servant, safely home. However, if I am unable to return, may you reign forever, and our enemies tremble in fear of your strength.'"

Avtandil paused as the advisor wrote his words on parchment. When Ustasra finished writing, he continued speaking.

"My speech has grown short, and so has the time between us. Now, I ask you to share my words with the King. Do this now, before others tell him of my departure."

"Summon your courage and speak to he who reigns over and above us all. Your reward for this will be one thousand pieces of gold. You may take it as payment or a bribe, whichever you prefer to call it for the service you do in my name."

# CHAPTER 13 -

## THE WELL OF SORROW

The advisor stood and stared at Avtandil. He smiled before speaking to the young Knight and kneeled in front of him as he began.

"Personal gain is not a disagreeable thing to me but keep your bribes for now. You found the road to me, and this is enough. Yet, I must ask how you believe I can tell the King what you have shared with me. It is the wisdom of many on which advice is carried to our Lord, and I am but one."

"I can say many things to him which would cause him to fill me with favors, but when he hears this news, he will ask how I can say these words to him. All the court will question why I am such a mad man to speak to Rostevan in this way. I do not doubt he will wait one moment before separating me from my head."

"You ask me to sacrifice all I have and lay my life down for your cause in exchange for a bribe. But nothing one man can give another is equal to the value of his life. To live is better than any treasure. As such, this thing cannot be said. It is impossible. A road cannot go over itself, nor can it go farther than it is, yet this is what you ask of me."

"No luck will carry me safely past the delivery of this news. Your words will not keep me whole, and the gold will remain in your hands. My reward will be the earth for a home."

"But what if the King does agree to your departure? Why should the hosts of our armies be deceived? They stand against our foes because you are their leader."

"The last time you left, it was kept secret. Do you think this secret will keep another three years? If you leave again the enemies on our frontiers will grow bold and array themselves against us. They will bring war upon our Kingdom. The King will never allow this to come to pass."

"You know our enemies have no power to stand against us as they are now, for sparrows cannot change into hawks. Yet, your actions would cause this impossibility to become a reality. You would gift our foe the strength needed to take the crown of Arabia."

A mix of pain and dismay colored Avtandil's face as he listened. Though it hurt him to do so, he pleaded once more with Ustasra, begging the advisor to understand his plight.

"I hoped to find a way forward through your wisdom. Yet, if you can find no road around the difficulties you speak of, how can I? Looking at you, I see a man who perhaps does not know what love is. Have you not seen the truth of friendship in others?"

"If you have seen these things, how can you expect me to find joy in doing nothing? I promised my brother Tariel to return. There is no other way for me. Should I push a knife into my heart for you to see this?"

"To my eyes, he shines like the Heavens. Although I

do not know how a man might aid one such as he, we must find a way to help him. For, in helping the sun, will it not also warm our days? I know you do not agree with what I am asking, but no one understands my affairs better than me. I am the only person who can say what is bitter or sweet to me."

"But these things do not matter now. You and I cannot stand here and do nothing but talk. We must do something. For the chatter of idle men truly grieves an honest man's heart. Let us speak truly of this."

"What benefit do you believe I will offer the King or our armies in my current state of mind? I am mad with desire to fulfill my duty and keep the promises I made to Tariel. Until then, nothing I can do will be of use to anyone in Arabia."

"I refuse to betray my brother or break my word, for oaths prove the worth of a man. Yet I think you have never experienced grief. And no man can truly understand something he has not seen."

"Still, I cannot believe you as an advisor could be so callous at this news. Is your heart cursed? If I were in your place, my heart would become like wax and not be so hard as stone. How else would you advise I repay the tears shed on behalf of my oath? Were the river Gihon or any other of Eden's four rivers to flow from my eyes, I could never pay such a debt."

"Truly, I say to you, if you would have help from me, it is help from you I must have. You worry about the frontier, which you fear will be at risk in my absence. Yet, I assure you, my men will not waver. Nor will I."

"If the King does not allow me to leave, I will go like a thief in the night. I will leave our Kingdom without anyone knowing the time or place of my departure. This is how it must be, for my vows consume me."

"For your part, I am sure the King will do nothing to

you because of me. I do not believe he will exile you, but if he does not see reason, I will sacrifice myself and suffer whatever torture Fate may lay upon you. Help me, and in doing so, help yourself."

The young man's words moved the stoic heart of the old advisor. His face flushed, and at last, he offered an answer Avtandil was willing to hear.

"Your sorrow moves me, and I cannot continue staring into the well of it. When I contemplate the depth of your suffering, the world itself vanishes from my eyes. You are correct, at least in part. Sometimes speech is better than silence. But sometimes, by speaking, we spoil things."

"I will present your case to the King. If I die, it is my fate, for I feel I must sacrifice my life to aid your cause. However, should your cause bring me to ruin and I yet live, your bribe shall be due to me."

With a short bow, Ustasra turned and left. The old advisor made his way to Rostevan's palace with measured and careful steps. As he drew closer, he considered which words would best carry the message he must deliver.

# CHAPTER 14 –

## THE WRATH OF A KING

U stasra was immediately brought to the King when he arrived. He was second only to Sograt among the wise men of Arabia, and everyone knew who he was. When he walked in, Rostevan came towards him, his face shining.

The advisor immediately understood his mistake when looking at the King's face. Rostevan's thoughts were not on matters of war. Instead, his sunny mood was occupied with pleasant things. Seeing this, the boldness of Ustasra's courage evaporated like morning mist. He was afraid to displease the King with unpleasant news. Not knowing what to do, he stood like a statue.

Greeting his advisor, Rostevan was surprised to see the man's hesitation. His joy turned to confusion and from there to concern. He understood there must be some problem he was unaware of and addressed the man with sharp and direct words.

"What is wrong with you? Why do you come before me with a face of stone and sorrow? You are a wise man. Such concern must mean you have no small news to share with me. Tell me what it is now, without delay."

Ustasra was caught like a hare in a trap. Too late, he realized the folly of his arrogance. He answered with a trembling voice.

"My Lord, in your presence, I realize I know nothing. Any apology I might make will neither add to nor surpass my own grief. But I am indeed sad, for you may choose to slay me when you hear what I have to say. However, it is the duty of an envoy to have no care for fear."

With these words, the advisor carefully told the King all he knew of Avtandil and his plans to leave. When he finished the story, he offered a few words in closing.

"Mere words are not sufficient to express the sorrowful state of the Knight. In my arrogance, I believed myself capable of explaining something a lifetime of learning has left me barely able to grasp. I know now you will be justified if your wrath falls upon my head."

He stared down at the floor when he finished speaking, counting the seconds until they bent into minutes. At last, he heard the King's voice, though it shook with barely contained rage.

"Where has your mind gone? How is it this news has turned you into a madman? Who else would have dared to share this with me? It is a bad man who chooses to learn early of what is evil."

"You come before me like a traitor and share something there is no joy to be found in. What more could someone do to hurt me other than perhaps leave me without faith and treacherously stab me in the back. You must be crazy to use your tongue with such disregard against me."

"A loyal man has a duty to spare his Lord such terrible news. How can you not know this? Yet you, like an old and toothless gossip, stupidly chatter this misery in my presence. Had I known of your coming, I would beg God to deafen my ears before your idiocy forced me to hear what you have said. And now, if I kill you, I will bear the responsibility of your blood."

"I swear to you, if it was not Avtandil who sent you to me, I would separate your head from your body with my own hands. Do not doubt this. Now, get away from me! Go from here and let all around me see the mad and stupid man you are!"

"Let anyone so foolish as to follow you from the cliffs of folly do so! Your brash and arrogant bravery is an affront to my eyes, and you are not worthy of being here. Not as an advisor nor even as a stable hand!"

In a rage, the mighty King began picking up the furniture closest to him and throwing it at the advisor. Ustasra ducked his head in fear as heavy and gilded chairs hit the walls, splintering into pieces around him.

Then he turned and ran like a fox caught entering a henhouse. By blind luck, he escaped death, but shame at his actions would forever haunt his days. The King's angry words chased his steps as he escaped.

"How could you tell me my foster son departs Arabia once more? He was grown in the garden of Eden and has braided the willow tree of my life. Who are you to dare share this black news with me in such a casual manner!"

The sounds of breaking wood and glass receded into the distance as Ustasra fled. He had entered the palace as a respected man, and now he was shamed. The mud and dirt of his disrespect soiled his thoughts like dirt on a potato seller come straight from the fields and to the market.

He felt like his tongue had dishonored him by bringing the King's anger down on his head. But in truth it was his own greedy hands grasping at Avtandil's gold which did the deed. For no man can hurt another more than he is able to hurt himself.

He chastised himself with each step, complaining at how shortsighted greed had made him. In truth, he hoped his words would offer some consolation to his tattered pride and bruised ego.

"Why did I let the sorrow of Avtandil darken my sight until I deceived myself into this foolishness? There is no evil God could possibly punish me with which I have not already done for myself. I am twice the fool for my arrogance, as I did not seek the counsel of my own advisors before speaking with the King."

"Any man so stupid as to behave like me deserves his fate. Now the evil of my words will hang about Rostevan's neck like a stone, and I will carry this burden for all my days! Yet at least I will receive the agreed payment, which I have surely earned. Perhaps I may make a better road with those coins than the one I have built today."

# CHAPTER 15 -

## THE SERVANT'S MESSAGE

Though he brought it on himself, Ustasra cursed his bad luck and misfortune. He returned to the house of Sograt, where he told Avtandil what happened in the palace. His face was sad as he began speaking.

"What thanks can I give you! I have become less than a courtier for my service to you. The honor and stature I once held are brought to nothing. I will not repeat what the King said to me, but it is enough for you to know he considers me a madman. He attributed such evil and stupidity to me as I've never heard him speak before."

"I am amazed he did not slay me where I stood. Perhaps, as I no longer deserve to be called a man, God gave him patience, and he took pity on me. But what can I say? I am ruined."

"I knew what I did and understood he would be furious with me. My actions were no mistake, which only increases my grief. As a wise man, I should have known better than to involve myself in the doing of this deed."

"However, what I did is finished now. My fate is sealed, as none can avoid vengeance for an evil thing done with forethought. Still, death would be a joy to me for your sake, so my woe is not in vain. But without your gold, perhaps I would not have agreed at all."

Then he lifted his eyes and smiled. This was the same smile Avtandil had first seen when he spoke to the advisor. In that moment, he understood the truth of the man's heart.

With a laugh, Ustasra clapped his hands, summoning servants to bring wine as he reminded the young Knight of his promise.

"As I recall, the matter of one thousand gold pieces remains unsettled between us, though, I am sure I need not remind you. You are aware of the Mourav, who is the chief arbitrator of debts. No doubt you know those who do not settle what they owe are sure to be caught by his long arms. And as the sages teach, a bribe settles matters even in Hell. At least with your gold, I will have something as compensation for what I have sacrificed."

The Knight, being a man of his word, made Ustasra's payment. Oaths and promises were no small matter to him, but his heart remained unsettled. Not satisfied with the King's answer, he continued discussing his problem.

"It is clear to me that Rostevan still disagrees with my departure, but I will not remain in Arabia. I can have no rest until my vows to Tariel have been settled. If I cannot do this, I will roam the fields and forests with wild beasts."

"Why would our King want me to fight our enemies if I am in such a state? It is better to have no man than a dissatisfied one. You should have told him this! When a rose withers, the nightingale dies of a broken heart. His only hope is to find a dewdrop of water. Even if he must go everywhere until he finds it, nothing else can soothe him."

"I will tell the King myself, and however angry he is, I pray he will see how I am consumed by the flames of devotion. If he will not agree, all I hope for is gone. There will be no choice for me but to make my own way. I will leave in the night, though my village may be uprooted, and wealth lost."

Unable to find words to offer the Knight, the wise man could only agree with him. They talked more, and the advisor made a banquet in honor of Avtandil. He made gifts to those who came, and the Knight returned home as the sun was setting. His course was set, though he did not yet know how it might end.

When he entered his chambers, he sat down to prepare his last plea to Rostevan. With a careful hand, he wrote these words.

"My King, you are both Lord and father to me. I cannot think of how to give sufficient praise of you and your accomplishments. Nor can I think of anything I might give you equal to the debts I owe for all you have done and given me. But I need to leave. I cannot sit idle while my oath makes a mockery of me."

"I sent Ustasra to speak on my behalf, for Sograt is far from the Kingdom. Yet, he could not convince you of my desire. Now, I ask once more for your blessing. This is a thing I must do. I have no other way."

"If I survive, I will die for you a thousand times. I will be your slave and repay your love with a love of equal weight. But now I must go."

"I am sending this message to ask for your permission again. But with or without your approval, I will leave for Tariel an hour before the sun rises. May God give me your answer before this time."

Having written his message to the King, the young

Knight rolled the parchment and sealed it with hot wax, affixing the seal of his ring as he did do. When he finished, he summoned two men to his rooms. One man was sent to bring Shermadin, his childhood companion and fellow Knight. For, when a man is in trouble, he most needs a brother and a friend.

Avtandil gave the other man the letter, commanding him to deliver it directly to the King. If Rostevan was busy, the servant was to wait like an envoy until he could complete the task. However, should the message be undelivered by morning, he was to burn it.

Not long after the men left, Shermadin arrived. He was breathless and brimming with concern over the late hour of his summons. When he saw the mental state of his friend, he immediately embraced him, asking how he could help.

# CHAPTER 16 –

## THIS IS THE WAY

Avtandil held his friend's embrace for a moment and then stepped back. He asked Shermadin to sit and then took the seat opposite him. With a weary sigh, he began his tale.

"My dear friend, you, who have so often comforted my heart, are the first hope I have had this day. Though it pains me, I must ask a dreadful thing of you. It is something I hoped to never request again. Yet, my time in Arabia is shortened. I can do nothing to change what must be done."

"Rostevan did not grant me leave to keep my vows. He did not listen to a word of what I asked. I fear he cannot understand how I have lost myself to another, yet it is true. Without Tariel, I have no life. If I do not return to him, no home is left to me, whether here or elsewhere."

"I swore an oath and cannot break it. My decision is final. For those people who lie are traitors and insult God.

In doing so, they betray He on High. I am a man of honor and no liar. But more, I can find no joy in knowing how another friend suffers alone. Surely you understand this, for you are equally my brother."

"You know the three ways of showing friendship. First is the wish to spend time together, coupled with longing in the absence of those dear to the heart. The second is always being generous and giving without growing weary or tired. Third, one must always be willing to roam the fields and provide attention and aid in times of need."

"But I fear I waste time to no end now. I would stay if there was another way, but I have found none which are open to me. What need do I have to lengthen my speech? Now is the time to shorten it."

"I will leave Arabia tonight, and the journey will heal my bruised heart. I only ask you to listen now and do as I command. You must once more fortify our Kingdom, doing those things I have already taught you."

"Prepare yourself to serve the Lords in my absence. You will be the first leader while I am gone, for no one is more capable than you. I leave the fate of Arabia in your hands and need you to command our troops and show valor in all you do."

"Battle the enemies on the edges of our frontiers and keep them from the gates. Remember to be kind with those who are loyal but slay the ones who show themselves to be traitorous and false. I will reward you greatly if I return, for service to a master is never lost. This, my friend, is what you must do for me."

Shermadin could not believe what he was hearing. His friend had been gone three years, and not even a week had passed since he returned home. Now he would leave to roam the fields alone again. Though he loved Avtandil, it was more than he could bear to hear.

"I have no fear of sorrow or loneliness when you are

near, but now you plan to leave again. What will I do in your absence? Twilight will fall over my heart like a funeral shroud. You cannot understand what these last years have been like. I stared from the walls of our frontier every morning and every evening in the hopes of seeing you, and now you're leaving again. Why can't you take me with you, and why must you always go alone?"

"Who has heard of one Knight wandering the fields so often and far as you? In all the world, I am unaware of another who does this. You have said how useless you will be to Rostevan, but what of me? Do you think I will be of any more use, knowing you are gone? What kind of Knight are you asking me to be? One who holds back from helping his own friend in time of need?"

Avtandil's eyes lit with a smile. The devotion of his lifelong friend moved him. He took the hands of Shermadin and spoke softly.

"You who have stood by me through my every joy and tragedy are like none other. But however much it pains you, I am unable to take you with me. Fate has once again taken up arms against me. I am besieged from all sides and can only trust you to do these things in my absence."

"I would have no other by my side if there was any other cause for my pain. Yet, I am at once a lover and at the same time forsaken by love. My heart runs wild, and so I must roam the fields alone. You must realize errantry is the business of lovers. One should not wait until he is old or the flower of life fades. This is how it is, and we must all submit to the world's will or be consumed by our own designs."

"Be sure my thoughts will be close when I am far from you. I fear no enemy and can take care of myself, but a brave man must not allow himself to drown in grief. He cannot falter when the world does not move in step with him. This is the way."

"You and I are Knights, and we each have our responsibilities, but we are also men and must keep ourselves whole and happy. This is the reason I need to go. If I stay, I will become an old man before my time. All my days will rot like grapes left too long on the vine. In the sun of my old age, I will be left gathering cucumbers and courting death."

"Understand what I say, for I have already told you of my love for Tinatin. To leave here is to abandon her whom I have been in service to these many years away. I have not enjoyed my time alone or the absence of her. Yet, if my sun has given me her blessing, why should I stay longer?"

"I realize this hurts you, but your service to me as a Knight lies in doing what I ask of you. I will address Rostevan in a letter, which I will leave in your care. Therein will be my instructions and requests. Therein, I will ask him to care for you as he has cared for me."

"Of you, I will ask only you not to slay yourself if I die. This is the deed of Satan. Do not do it. Instead, weep for me. Let your eyes run rivers and remember the brother and friend I have been to you."

# CHAPTER 17 –

## NEITHER APOSTLE NOR SAINT

With these words, Avtandil turned from Shermadin and sat at his desk. He began the painful process of composing a letter for Rostevan. It was as if the ink were dipped from his own blood and each line of every word highlighted in the agony he felt.

"My King, I write these words to you with a pitiful and trembling hand. You have undoubtedly heard of my plight and the heart which beckons me from afar. I am unable to deny him, so I have stolen away like a thief in the night. This is shameful, but I pray you will forgive me and be merciful, remembering how God behaves towards those who are lost in the fires of love and devotion."

"In the end, Fate traps us all in her weave, though I hope you will not blame my resolve. A wise man cannot abandon his beloved. But more, I would remember the wisdom and wit of Aristotle, Plato, and Socrates, which you taught me as a boy. From those lessons, I understood falsehood and bearing two faces are lies which first injure the mind, and then the soul."

"I carry these words with me as I leave, though I am pained near death to be separated from you and my beloved Arabia. Yet, since lying is the source of all misfortune, I cannot forsake my friend. I am not a King like you and have no throne to uphold. Save that which exists in a bond stronger than brothers."

"But my pen grows long with these thoughts. They are not what I would say to you. I find no succor in repeating the ideas of philosophers. We are all taught that one day we may be united with the hosts of Heaven, but before those days pass, God has given us free will. Yet, I have no choice but to do this thing. My only wish is to find words which will help you understand what is in my heart."

"You have read of the apostles and how they speak of love, yet I feel those words were written in another time. Sages tell us lovers are exalted by their feelings, but for some, the song remains unheard. It is no more than the ringing of distant bells. If one does not hear the song, how can they imagine the truth?"

"I am no apostle. Nor am I a saint. What one man does not understand, I cannot show him, for he is ignorant. Such a man has not seen the light of He who created me and does not recognize the invisible might which is the aid of every earthly being. It is our God who fixes the bounds of the finite and sits immortal above us. In one moment, he can change a hundred into one, or one to a hundred."

"We believe all things are eternal in Heaven, but on this world, they are not. Our sun is the face of God for roses and violets, yet they fade and die if they cannot gaze on the glory of their Lord. Not only them, but also everything else desirable. All things are brought to ruin without the touch of His hand. For me, Tariel has become like this light. How can I endure separation from him?

What pleasure will my life have if I am denied his presence?"

"However angry you may be when you read these words, I hope you will find room in your heart to forgive me for not keeping your commands. No power remained in my heart, for I have become enthralled by this Knight in the Panther Skin. My only choice was to leave Arabia. I have no other remedy for the fires raging in me."

"In the end, it does it matter where I am if my free will has been taken. Knowing this, do not be sad because I have gone. I could not avoid it, for duty is the unwritten law between true men. All of us struggle and suffer woe, yet none have the power to thwart the will of Heaven."

"I must ask you to allow my road to be whatever God has set before me. Let this thing come to pass, so I may fulfill my destiny. When I return, my soul will no longer be a grave of ash. In my heart, I hope to return and see you joyful and enjoying wealth of all types. For me, whatever I do in His name is sufficient glory. I can ask no more."

"This is my decision. Though it pains me to no end knowing my departure causes you grief, I have no alternative. I cannot speak falsely or abandon my oaths like a coward. He who reigns high would shame me when we meet in the eternity where we will end our days. Slay me if any can deny the truth of these words."

Avtandil stopped writing for a moment and thought about the weight of what he was trying to say. He understood how deeply his words would hurt Rostevan, but he had no choice. Carefully considering what he would say next, he dipped his pen into the ink once more and continued.

# CHAPTER 18 -

## IN MY STEAD

"Those mindful of their friends will not bring uninvited harm to one another. They are not false like treacherous liars who trade in shame. But ask yourself, what is worse than a hesitant and timid man who is forever late? I cannot become someone like this. Not even for a mighty King such as you. If I do not keep my vows, I am nothing."

"You know this to be true! But I still feel my tale is one of shame. My only wish was to see you once more before I left, but I understood you would not give me leave to depart Arabia. I cannot become a coward for my service to you, for there is no worse man than one in a fight who frowns and hides out fear of death."

"What would I do? Sit idly and weave webs of gossip like a lonely widow? It is a far better choice to seek glory than possessions. We are men and must behave as such."

"No matter how narrow the road, it cannot keep death

at bay. Nor will strewing rocks and stones across the path slow the procession of time. All fortifications are leveled by Him, whether weak or strong. In the end, youthful and greybeards alike are gathered in the same place. Because of this, a glorious death is better than a shameful life!"

"You know this thing which unites us all comes without fail, whether by day or night. Those who do not expect death in a moment are mistaken, and especially they who are warriors, for the way of a warrior is death."

"Though it pains me to write this, I must remind you how fleeting life is. Though it is a difficult thing to ask, have pity on my soul if I am consumed by Fate, the destroyer of all. Be tender and merciful towards me in your prayers. Know that all I would have wished from He on High is one more day in your grace."

"Release my servants. Enrich them with my lands and give what treasure remains to those who are poor. Make an orphanage of my home, for I would die traveling as an orphan and be mourned by none wherever I fell. Yet, those without means will forever be grateful to me."

"They will bless my name. In this way I will be remembered by those who came from the same beginnings as me. Because of this I would also ask you to build bridges for the poor and burdened of this earth. Let my death aid those who have nothing."

"If I fail, there are none but you who can carry me from the fires of Purgatory. For I will no longer have any way of giving you news of my comings and goings. With these writings, I commit my soul to you. No deeds of the Devil will seduce me, and I will prevail over every evil and forever remain true to Arabia."

"Forgive me my trespasses and offer your prayers for my safe return. Whatever debts may lie between us at my departure, they are will not matter until I have returned, for a dead man cannot pay what is owed. Pray I return to settle my affairs with you, my beloved father."

"In my stead, I have chosen Shermadin to represent me. This duty burdens him with grief greater than I gifted him before. Please be kind and gentle in your commands to him. Give him your favor, for I would not have his loyalty repaid with tears and sharp words."

"These words are the sum and end of my testament. It is written by my hand and affixed with my seal. As you read this, I have left, for I can have no home until my oaths are kept. Separation from Tariel maddens my heart."

"Do not let the Lords grieve my passing. Refrain from draping yourselves in gloom. Instead, be proud and fierce, for this is the face of the father I know and love. Let your sovereignty be feared by our foes, for we are Arabian!"

With this, Avtandil finished his letter to King Rostevan. He gave it to Shermadin before embracing his friend once more.

"Now, I must prepare myself. Soon I will depart our lands for the unknown. Though I cannot tell you when I might return, you will forever be on my mind as I roam. Please, give this letter to the King, but use discretion. Only you have the strength to complete the tasks I ask and do what must be done in my absence."

An hour before dawn, Avtandil saw no sign of the messenger he sent to Rostevan. So, he readied himself to leave. The road to Tariel would be long and difficult, and he set his heart and mind to the task before him. Kneeling in prayer, he asked for the blessing of Heaven.

"Mighty God, who rules the earth below and Heavens above, I pray you will give me strength to carry my burdens and endure the longing in my heart. At once, these things beg me to stay and to go. I know you forever lift the hearts of those who are deserving, yet I am also aware of your punishments to the false and treacherous."

"This day, I am neither. Fate has left me adrift in a sea of uncertainty. I cannot say if I come or go. Nor do I know where I might rest. All I am certain of is that I must depart the lands of my home to help another in need."

"I have none other than You, our merciful Lord, to whom I might beg for aid on the paths ahead of me. All I ask is Your favor. However far or long I may travel, shelter me from the mastery of my foes. Keep me safe from the turmoil of the seas and deliver me from the darkness which comes in the night."

"Help me find my way safely home and carry me through any evil which may rise against me. Please grant me this wish, for it is all I ask. I am now and forever your servant. May the glory of Heaven shine upon my soul."

When he finished his prayers, he turned towards the palace. With sorrow, he bowed towards Rostevan, whispering a few last words out of respect and honor for the King he knew as a father.

"I thank you, who took me into your home when I had no other to raise me. Though it is not my wish to leave your side, I go now. The world beckons me to an end I cannot predict, and for all my strength, I have no power in me to resist the call of this siren. I wish you strength and health in my absence and hope to return and look upon your shining face again one day."

After speaking, the Knight turned away and mounted his horse, riding off into the distance. His friend and loyal vassal watched as the youth disappeared into the distance. Despite wanting to follow Avtandil, the weight of service bound Shermadin stronger than any chains. He could not forsake his duty to Arabia, nor his friend. Each day he would protect and serve the people while praying for the safe return of his Lord.

# CHAPTER 19 –

## WHERE EAGLES DARE

In the morning, Rostevan woke in a foul mood. His mind still warred with the news Ustasra had given him. Though he sat in the audience hall, it remained empty of visitors. None were willing to risk his wrath with petty matters and squabbles.

Yet, empty chambers and reticent visitors would not console him. His face appeared to pour flame upon those few who were forced into his presence. Unsatisfied with how he felt, the King commanded the treacherous advisor to be brought before him.

Ustasra was enjoying himself. The man was full of cheer after his celebration with Avtandil the day before. But he went pale with fear when informed of the King's summons. Escorted to the palace, concern etched his face as guards brought him into the audience hall.

Looking at him, Rostevan carefully considered what to say before speaking, mindful of his brewing anger.

"Yesterday, you came to me with the manners of a goat

herder. I cannot recall what you said, but I remember being angry. My soul could not find peace or composure. Though I scolded you, I am certain my actions had merit."

"You caught me unawares with your words, and I do not remember what Avtandil wanted or why I treated you so poorly. Tell me what you said yesterday but be honest. Select your words carefully, for spite is a net of woes."

At first, the advisor was hesitant, choosing his words with the utmost care. But Rostevan's calm demeanor gave him courage. Ustasra hoped to regain favor, and soon repeated the whole story. When he finished, the King spoke once more, but only shortly.

"If I do not believe you are a madman now, may God cause me to be cursed for my anger, like the Jew Levi. My reaction yesterday was not wrong. I do not want to hear more from you about this. Go and bring Avtandil to me before I give up any consideration of your redemption!"

The wise man left and searched for Avtandil. He went everywhere until coming to the Knight's home. There, he found the house in chaos. Servants were wandering around, uncertain what they should do, and messengers waited at the entrance without being received. Ustasra quickly realized what had happened and left, muttering to himself as he went.

"The Knight is gone, no doubt like a thief in the night. This much is certain from the state of his house. If I return, the King will surely have my head this time. Already, I wish I had not spoken so boldly before. Let someone else give him this news. Whoever is daring, let him dare."

When the advisor did not return, Rostevan sent one of his men to summon Avtandil. However, when the man learned the Knight was no longer in the Kingdom, he paled. Afraid to return with such news, he waited outside the palace. As the hours passed, more people came looking for their Hero, yet none dared to ask. Soon, rumors began.

It did not take the King long to suspect the truth. He bowed his head in thought and calmed himself. After a few deep breaths, he called another messenger to his side.

"Go and bring the villain Ustasra to me. He is to appear without delay. Any hesitation will be at his own peril. Do not fail me in this."

When the wise man received the message, he returned to the audience chamber immediately. He was pale and afraid. The King spoke shortly to him, asking only one thing, to which he already suspected the answer.

"Has the sun gone away from us and become inconsistent, like the moon?"

With trembling speech, the wise man spoke, telling all he knew of how Avtandil had left in secret. He finished speaking with a sigh.

"It is true. The sun no longer shines on us. The skies are not bright today!"

Rostevan cried out as he heard this. He tore at his beard in frustration, shouting and lamenting his pain.

"What will become of me when I cannot see your joy in returning from the hunt or playing games in the courtyards and fields? How will I rest or enjoy any song when it is not accompanied by your sweet voice? All my days will be dark without the brightness of your stare. Where have you taken the shining pillars of light you look out at the world from?"

"No doubt your bow and hand will provide you sustenance, but what will become of me if I die? Who will stand with me in my final moments or mourn my passing? To be sure, wherever you have gone, no one will recognize you as the orphan took in and raised as my own."

"But I am your foster father. I remember. In your absence, my heart is gone with you. Now it is I who am orphaned until I see you again. No words can give justice to my suffering."

As the King's last words left his lips, a cry went up from the many Lords and courtiers who had gathered to learn news of Avtandil. Some cried, and others shouted, bemoaning the darkness they felt in the absence of the Hero of Arabia.

All at once, everyone began talking. Some wanted to go and find the Knight. Others were worried about what would happen to the Kingdom without their protector. In the end, Rostevan's voice cut through the noise.

"The sun has indeed made his rays quite rare to us. I do not know what we have done to annoy him or how we have sinned. More, I cannot say who will lead our armies in his absence. But you must tell me if he is alone, or has taken a squire with him?"

Seeing and hearing the commotion, Shermadin had come to the palace, and now walked through the crowd. He approached the King with a mix of fear and shame. Once again, he was forced to lie on behalf of his friend. As before, it cut him, but he would not betray his friend's trust. With an outstretched hand, he delivered Avtandil's letter to Rostevan and spoke.

"I found this letter in his chambers. It is addressed to you, my Lord. He left Arabia alone. Neither youth nor graybeard went with him. If you choose to slay me, it is deserving. Without him, life is devoid of joy."

Rostevan took the parchment and opened it. As he read what was written in the letter, he understood his foster son's burden. There was no joy in this knowledge but at least a measure of closure. He ordered widows and orphans to pray their Knight would find peace on his road and enjoy a safe and speedy return home. For the troops, he commanded them to dress in dark colors and mourn the sorrow now draped about the Kingdom.

# CHAPTER 20 –

## GIVE ME YOUR AID

In the Kingdom of Georgia, far removed from Arabia, sages have written that when the moon is not near his sun, distance makes him glow brighter. Yet when the sun is near, her rays consume him. He is repelled and cannot approach her. The same is true of roses. They all wither and die without the sun's light but are consumed when it comes too close. People are the same, and not seeing those we love renews old grief. Like a rose or a moon in the darkness, they lose their color.

Avtandil was no different. Though the brightness of Heaven shone on his pale form, he was heartsick. Every hill he crossed brought him closer to Tariel, but his pain increased with each step. Often, he looked back over his shoulder in the hopes of finding his love looking at him. Yet only the long road stretched out behind him.

She was not there. As the emptiness around him grew, so did the expanse of sorrow draped over his heart. He complained to Fate as he rode, hoping the words would lessen the weight of his oaths.

"The space between us stretches over me like a curse. Though I am farther away with the passing of every hour, my mind remains with you. Why can't my heart return to you, or my eyes, so I might see you again? A lover should be the subject of his or her love, but I am absent. Instead, the arms of duty embrace me like a vise."

The days passed slowly for him. It seemed he rode through eternity, one step chasing another. Every night he rejoiced at the rising of the moon and appearance of the stars. They reminded him of Tinatin, and he called to them in her name, speaking to the full moon as he did.

"In the name of Heaven, I plead, for it is you who gives the plague of love to lovers. Yet, in the brightness of your gaze, they find a salve to soothe their hurts and guide them. Listen to my prayers and unite me once more with the sun of my life, she of the fair face and raven hair."

During the day, he would ride on, but as time passed, he began to despise the light. Its brightness added to the flames consuming his heart. He felt more tortured with every new sunrise and longed for the sunset. Soon he made his road one of twilight, bidding farewell to the day.

"My sun, whom the greatest of philosophers have addressed as God. I ask you to hear my words. You are everlasting, and every heavenly body submits to your will. I pray you will continue to shine on me, though I may see little of you in the coming weeks."

"It is true, I count the moments until I meet the woman I love by your rays, yet each one pierces me like a lance. Give me your aid, for I am captive. Chains of iron bind me. Before, I could not endure the nearness of my love, but I now lament her absence. Carry us with your light until she and I are together again."

As he spoke his last words, the sun dipped below the

sky in a fiery sunset of gold and copper. When the night came, he rejoiced and rode on. In time he found a stream at the edge of a vast plain. He dismounted at the water's edge and stared at the moonlight reflecting from it. Among the rocks on the far side, he spotted a goat, which was soon cooking over his fire.

As he roasted the meat, he thought about what was before and behind him. His love was far, and he farther with each night, which pained him. But the plight of Asmath and Tariel also raked coals across his soul, and they were in the opposite direction from Tinatin. It was not the way of a Knight to abandon those he loved, yet here he was, caught between the space of all he loved.

He had forsaken the rose of his heart to keep an oath to his brother and sister. Now the caves of the Devi had become something of a waypoint to him. Whatever happened, he had no choice but to carry on. The events of his life were not yet decided by Fate, and he did not want the suffering of those he loved to have been for nothing.

Marshalling his emotions and settling his mind, he turned his attention to finishing his cooking, continuing to think about life. He knew having joy in one hand would not fill the other, but both of his hands were empty without Tinatin or the friends he journeyed towards. However, his destination was not too far off.

When he walked up to the cliffs and saw his friends again, joy would be in his grasp once more. But first, he needed to eat. He would need his strength for the road ahead.

# CHAPTER 21 –

## THE BRAND OF BETRAYAL

With each passing night Avtandil drew closer to his destination, traveling over hills and valleys. He arrived one morning, when the sun was barely a hand high in the sky. His heart sang with joy as the cliffs came into view, and he rode up to entrance of the caves without pause.

Asmath heard a horse approaching and ran out. When she saw it was her lost brother, she was unable to contain her happiness. He jumped down from his horse, and they embraced. For when someone has waited for another, their coming is full of joy.

Looking around, Avtandil noticed Tariel had not come out, and he asked whether his brother was resting or had not yet returned from one of his hunts. Yet, the maiden started sobbing. Through her tears, she told all she knew.

"When you left, he grew restless, like a caged lion. In time, he began to roam the wilds. At first, a little, but then more. You have seen how he is, impatient sometimes and angry others. It irritated him to wait and do nothing in your absence."

"Two weeks have passed, and I have no news of him, nor sight or sign. He has not returned, and I cannot tell you what has become of him or where he went!"

Avtandil stared at her with surprise. He heard what she said, but believing it was another matter. Her words shocked him to the core of his being.

"This is not the way of a Knight! It is a black thing for him to break an oath with his sworn brother. Why did he promise me if he was not planning keep his word? How could he lie to me like this and leave?"

"I did not deceive him in any way. For him, I left my love and an entire Kingdom behind. I willingly cast all my life to the winds and counted a world of grief as the cost. Everything I had is now in shambles. Without him, what did I do this for? I don't understand why he would break his vow, but Fate's evil should not surprise me."

The maiden put a hand on his arm, trying to calm him. She spoke and he listened, though the hurt he carried remained etched across his face.

"Your sorrow is justified. This much is certainly true, but you still have life in you. He does not. Though I have not been complacent in your absence, nothing I might have done would have stopped him from going out."

"The heart, mind, and thoughts of any person are all dependent on one another. If even one fails or is taken from a man, the others will soon follow. He is no different. Deprived of his heart, Tariel has become less than a shadow. He can't play the part of a man anymore."

"Woe and pain caused him to be chased away from any resemblance to men. You know every man needs an intact heart to fulfill his promises. Yet, the last time you were here, you brought him back from the edge of his abyss with your own heart. So perhaps it was your heart with which he made those oaths."

"Whatever pain you carry, you did not see and cannot truly comprehend the fires consuming him. You are still alive. Your heart beats, but he only waits for the end of his days."

"It is right for you to complain about his absence. I am sure separation from your sworn brother must bruise your soul, but I tell you again. You did not see how broken he was these last weeks. To my sorrow, I have always been there to witness his agony."

"Other than you, only one other knows the tale of his suffering. But what you understand from a book is different than what you learn on the battlefield. You spent three years in search of something God gave you the grace to find. Yet he has been lost more than twice this time."

"I am unable to imagine the pain he endures. My tongue would fail if I tried to give voice to it. I would succumb to exhaustion and only gift myself further heartache. No ordinary man could shoulder the burden of his tragedy. Stones have split for less, and the tears he cries could make a fountain to last an eternity."

"Still, what you said before remains true. One is wise in the battles of another. While he was wrong to leave, I hope he still breathes. When he went away from here, it was as if flames enveloped him. He was so hot I was unable to approach."

"I asked what I would say when you returned. He spoke at length before leaving and said, 'I am useless to the world now. Tell him to come and find me, for I will not travel far from here. My oath will be kept, but I must roam from here or be lost forever.'

"'Wherever my steps carry me, it is there I will be. For the sake of Avtandil, I will wait. Though I cannot say what he will find on his arrival.'"

"'If he finds me dead, let him bury me. Ask him to mourn the man I once was and forgive the one I have become. If I am still breathing by some chance, may he celebrate the miracle of my existence. Offer thanks to God, for perhaps there is still some hope in this world.'"

"'For me, the sun is split. My body lies crushed beneath the mountain of duty, and I cannot move. Every breath I take is torture to my soul. My groans of pain go unanswered. Death has forgotten me, and Fate continues her evil ways.'"

"'At the last, I would say only this. In the Eastern Kingdoms of China, one stone holds barely legible words of wisdom carved into it. *He who does not seek the aid of friends is his own enemy.* This is a truth I have not forgotten. Nor have I forgotten the oaths and promises I swore to my brother. Let him seek me, though I turn the color of saffron, and fade faster than a violet.'"

With these words, Asmath finished all she had to say. She raised her eyes to Avtandil, tears still fresh on her cheeks, and waited to hear what he would do.

# CHAPTER 22 -

## LOST AND ALONE

After Asmath finished speaking, Avtandil considered what he knew and what she had said. First among these things was the truth of matters. It was true there was much he did not know about Tariel, but he did not believe such things mattered. Faithful men were always the equal of one another. However, he knew too well that loyalty was not a trait all men possessed.

Some clung to the lie of time and experience in trade for trust. Yet they were no more or less subject to the whims of Fate. One turn of events was all it took for them to be equally ruined and betray one another. But he and Tariel were Knights. They were a different class of men, and their hearts were true. So were their vows.

He would not abandon his friend. It wasn't something he considered. Though, he was a bit ashamed of thinking Tariel had betrayed him. He said as much to the maiden.

"It is right you did not justify my complaints against

our friend and brother. It was wrong of me to speak against him. But you must understand why I thought he broke his vows."

"My love for him has made me a prisoner serving his cause. The weight of my actions in Arabia bears down on me like a stone. I fled my home, and like a stag seeking water, I wandered from field to field in search of him."

"In the wake of my departure, Tinatin sits alone. I have gone away from her. Without Tariel, I was unable to bring her the happiness she deserved. Neither was I capable of finding my own happiness, for my thoughts were forever on him and you. Every step I took was chased with worry and concern for your well-being. Yet, in leaving, I have angered the equals of God."

"The favors I asked of friends and advisors deeply trouble their hearts. I have been faithless to my King and foster father. He who raised me when I was orphaned, who is merciful, sweet, and gentle towards me like snow falling from a soft sky. My service to him has been less than commendable, and I bear so much guilt I cannot speak of it. Surely no reward awaits me from God for what I have done."

"For Tariel's sake, all these things afflict me. I have become a man with no home. Like a wayfarer, I drift by night and day. Now, when I have come to find him, he is gone. I sit alone, wreathed in the fire of my pain, without knowing where he is. Therefore, you see me with such a sad face and sharp words."

"However, one must not try to catch the water which has passed under a bridge. The past is done, and there is nothing to repent. Now, I must not delay my search for him. The hour and time for me to leave are upon us, and we have no more space for conversation."

"I will find him and bring him here. My oaths will be fulfilled if he is alive, but if his death wish has been granted, Fate will have also doomed me. There will be nothing left I can say to God."

Avtandil took Asmath by the hands and then embraced her. He promised to return with Tariel or news of his fate. When they separated, he mounted his horse and turned away, riding past the rocks, over the water, and through the reeds bordering the path to the caves of the Devi.

Soon he was on the plains. A cold wind blew over the fields and froze his cheeks to a ruby hue. He spoke to himself as he rode, searching for any sign or track of his friend.

"Why does this plague from Fate endlessly hound my steps? Have I somehow sinned against God? I am separated from my friends, and it seems I've been lured into a black ending. Truly, if I die, no one will have pity on me. The blood of all I love will be on my own head."

"I am one, yet my every step is taken on behalf of two. My friend cast roses upon my heart. Yet he wounded me, for I have fulfilled the oath he did not keep. If he is truly lost to the world of men, all my joy will fade to dust."

"I will never again have friends without shame at the death of Tariel. It would be more fitting if God judged me in his place and shortened the length of my days on this earth. Yet, I hold hope he still lives. If all things are possible, then one must consider every possibility."

He rode over the plains in increasingly larger circles. With each new track, his distance from the caves grew. At the end of the day, he could not ride farther and rested under the open sky. As was his way, he counted each star in memory of Tinatin, praying to find his friend before it was too late.

The next day passed much like the first. By then he was far enough across the fields to have reached small thickets and reedy marshes. He called out and shouted as he searched, but never received any answer.

He rode like this for three days, until the entire plain became his track. Soon the marshlands gave way to hills and small patches of forest. Yet he still saw no sign of the man. As more days passed, sorrow and fear grew within him. They gnawed away at his resolve, causing his steps to become leaden. But he did not give up.

Three days were nothing to the three years he had once spent searching for the Knight in the Panther Skin. He could afford more time but wasn't sure if time was on his side. He found nothing that day, and it seemed all his days would be spent to no end.

# CHAPTER 23 –

## WHERE IS MY MIND

Unsatisfied and frustrated, he continued searching into the evening. When the plains were cast in a mix of sunlight and shadow and he was ready to give up, a black shape appeared in the distant reeds. Spurring his horse forward, he recognized Tariel's midnight steed.

Though there was no sign of the Knight, his heart leaped at the sight. He was overcome with joy and hope at the thought of finding his friend. Dismounting, Avtandil pushed through the tall reeds in search of his friend, calling and shouting. But there was no answer.

After a few steps, he came to a place where the foliage had been trampled into nothing. It looked as though a massive battle had occurred. Wary of danger, he cautiously stepped forward and found the ruined shape of Tariel lying in a heap on the ground.

Blood covered him and colored all the earth around where he had fallen. His head was torn and bitten, and his armor was ripped from the collar by the claws of something mighty. A bloody and broken sword was on one side of him, next to the corpse of a lion. On the other, a panther's twisted and broken body lay in a tattered heap.

It seemed the Knight had finally stepped away from the world of men. He stared with unblinking eyes, looking into the shadow realm his spirit journeyed towards. Yet, fresh water glistened on his cheeks. He cried, and so it appeared the man still lived. Avtandil did not know or care why Fate kept his brother caught between worlds. His only concern was preserving the candle flame by which Tariel clung to life.

Kneeling, he wiped the tears from the wounded Knight's eyes but received no response. He called his friend's name, cradling his head and trying to wake him. After what felt like an eternity, Tariel answered.

"Why do you disturb my rest? God has finally given me what I prayed for. I am only partially here, wrapped in the embrace of Death. The shadows of another landscape call me home. My vows are kept now. You have seen me."

"Now I must ask you to leave me to my rest. You know how Fate has abused me. I have beaten my head in vain for too many years. No man should endure the pain I suffer and not also die. Finally, I am at peace. I would only ask you to give my body a resting place. Bury me when I am gone, so the beasts do not desecrate my corpse."

His words confused Avtandil, for their promise was not to simply meet one another again. It was a vow sworn on the blood of brotherhood. They were bound forever to aid each other no matter the circumstances. Neither of them could forsake this duty and call himself a Knight.

Concerned by his friend's mental state, Avtandil took his hand and begged him to be reasonable.

"Where has your mind gone? What you do to me with these words is truly evil. And for what? Who has not been in love with another or been burned by the fires of their own hearts? Among all the men and their many races, none are living who can do what you are capable of. Yet your tongue has been seized by the Devil. Why else would you kill yourself by your own hand?"

"Your mind is healthy, yet you wrap bandages over your eyes and hide from reality. Each day you do this, your wounds are renewed, but you have closed your sight to the truth. Little wonder you have chosen to weep in the plains and live with wild beasts, yet this is not the way. While your agony blinds you to reality, you will never find any path to Nestan."

"I realize you are no fool, but the words of sages have fled your mind. Nothing worth having can come from seeking answers at the expense of yourself. If you will only lift your eyes from the sorrow drowning you, the way back to sanity will be clear. You find yourself in trouble through your own reasoning. Come back to us!"

"You know a man must be manly and weep as little as possible. In times of grief, he should strengthen himself like a stone wall. If not, who else will support those who rely on the solidity of his strength? Do you hear me? Are my words not enough for you to stand and come back to your vows and the needs of those who depend on you?"

# CHAPTER 24 –

## HOW WILL I LAUGH TOMORROW

Despite the intensity with which Avtandil spoke, Tariel did not answer him. Instead, he stared out from the world of the living and into the land of the dead. Desperate to revive his friend and force life back into him, Avtandil slapped his cheeks and shouted at him.

"Love has consumed us all equally! Who are you to believe yourself different? We all endure the fire of our devotions, but one man cannot fairly count his pain as more or less than another. You are no exception to this! Why should you allow your spirit to flee while we remain here to carry your burdens?"

"Do you think anyone has picked a rose without a thorn? No, they have not. If a rose could speak, it would tell you that none who try to capture its beauty do so without pain. For, though roses are without equal, there has never been one which did not hide thorns hide beneath its sweetness. The same is true of love, which you know!"

"If a soulless and inanimate rose would speak this way, what of men? Who among us can hope to harvest joy if

97

they have not first toiled in the fields? You and I are equally guilty of burdening Fate with responsibility for our failures and shortcomings. But what evil has it done that did not involve our own hands?"

"I tell you, nothing of value is without cost. What things are sweetest will always be found with the bitter. If having something lovely required no sacrifice, it would be cheapened. Its value would be no more than fruit left to rot beneath a forgotten tree."

"Listen to me and come away from this place. Do not follow your own counsel or do what you claim to desire. You are not thinking clearly and cannot decide what is best for you. Mount your horse and come at whatever pace you find comfortable, for it will not hurt you. Believe me, I would not suggest this if it would not help you. If you do not trust my words, ask yourself who has ever heard of a harmless thing which was the work of devilry?"

Tariel, somewhat roused from being slapped on the cheeks, stared up at his friend. His face was devoid of expression, and a small trickle of blood ran from the corner of his mouth as he answered Avtandil.

"Brother, there is nothing I can say. I barely have control of my own tongue. You believe the torment of my suffering has been easy, but madness grips me. What strength remains in me to truly understand your words? Death is near, and my prayers have been answered. The time of my release from this earth is close. I can feel it and welcome the grave with joy."

"My last thoughts will be of Nestan, who I will pray for. Though this life has parted us from one another, we may yet be united in the afterlife. In that place of shadows, perhaps we will meet one another and find some measure of the joy we were denied in this life. Can you not understand this?"

"What lover can go so long without seeing his love?

How can I forsake her, whom I have sought so many years? I will gladly go to her, and she will come to me. We will weep in each other's arms. She for me, and I for her. What need do you have for more questions? A hundred times I have asked, but now I will do what pleases my heart, despite what any may advise."

"These words are the truth, and this is my final decision. Though my spirit may wait at the wall which separates our worlds, it will not remain there long. The sun sets on me, so leave me alone. I am no use to you dead, and if I live a little longer, what can you do? The essence of my soul dissolves like dewdrops under the morning sun. Are you unable to understand me? I am no more."

"I don't understand what you have said, nor do I have the leisure to listen. Though you may think me mad, I can see the next world clearly. I understand now how this life is no more than a moment. It's a breath on the wind of time and then gone forever, like the flame of a candle, or one season into another."

"I do not mind losing this, for the world has grown more distasteful to me than at any other time. I am ready to leave, yet you disturb my rest. You ask me to hear you and understand the wisdom of men, but my eyes stare into eternity. Your words no longer matter."

"If I was whole, perhaps I would enjoy your speech, but how can a madman act wisely? How can you even ask? You know a rose cannot exist without sunlight, or it begins to fade. Do you not realize what you look on when your eyes rest on me? I am gone. Accept this and move on."

"Your talk wearies me. Leave, for I can endure no more of this. I have no time left in this world. Bury me and let the earth cover all I could not manage to be."

# CHAPTER 25 –

## MY HEART WILL BE FINE

Avtandil shouted in frustration, realizing his wisdom and kind words would not reach Tariel. There was nothing to be accomplished with speech. Instead, he must appeal to his friend's vanity if there was any hope of drawing him back from the grave.

"By my head! If the words I speak are empty to you, and there is nothing I might say to compel your return to the land of the living, so be it. It is a poor deed for me to mother a Knight who knows best for himself. Do what you will, but do not be your own foe."

"Since you will not listen to me, I will not tire my tongue further. If you long for death, then die. Let the rose of your form wither. For every rose eventually withers. I only ask you to pay attention to these last words of mine. After I have spoken, I will leave you to your grave, returning only to bury your body."

"Your passage from this world leaves me heartsore and

heart torn. When last we met, I was forced to leave your side in haste so I might go back to my love, Tinatin. Yet, I did not go quietly. Nor was I long in returning. Though you are unaware, my absence is mourned by a Kingdom and King who is a father to me."

"More, you have left nothing for me of the seeds we sowed across the field of our brotherhood. How can I speak of joy or find light when you have chosen to renounce me? I am left with no more than begging a farewell from you. At least grant me one wish, so I may remember you as you were and not the broken man who now departs the world of men."

"Mount your fine black steed and let me look once more on the glory of the last Prince of India. If you do this, my spirit will not be broken. In time my heart will heal from the loss of you, as all hearts must. But if you do not do this for me, my soul will never be whole again. Remember who you are and let this be your will!"

In truth, Avtandil did not care about seeing his friend on any horse, but he was out of options. Reason and wisdom had failed to help return his friend to the land of the living. But he knew stubbornness and vanity were as much a part of the Indian as the pain he carried. Beneath the man and behind his arrogance, a wounded soul cried out. This was the friend he loved, and he could not bring himself to abandon him.

If Tariel could be coerced into mounting his horse, he might be tricked into riding. When he saw the fields beneath him and looked across the plains, the bitter cold of his sorrow would flee. He would be saved, and the hand of death would loosen its grasp.

Without any sound or complaint, Tariel agreed to mount his black stallion once more. However, getting him in the saddle was difficult. The Indian was sorely wounded and had lost a great deal of his blood.

However, after much effort, Avtandil managed to get the wounded Knight seated. The, he led him and his horse a few steps away. He brought them towards the edge of the tall grass and mounted his own horse,

As they walked their horses, Avtandil spoke fair words. Each one was like a bird on the wing, or a star being born. Yet what he said was unique to the two brothers and could not be repeated. For when an Angel gifts a man with the speech of Heaven, the weight and meaning of those words are lost to any other. But listening to what they said at that moment would have made the ears of the old young again.

Intent on his friend's state of mind, Avtandil put away his sorrow and sadness. For, what is a friend if he does not put his grief aside to help those he loves? Instead, he was patient and kind.

The grief which had overcome Tariel began to fade. His complexion improved, and the rose of his cheeks showed the slightest of color. Kind words and fresh fields lifted his spirits, and a measure of his former self returned. He who had before spoken without sense began to talk reasonably.

This was the goal of Avtandil, for joy is the physician of the reasonable, while sighing and moaning are medicines of the foolish. But he desired more from his friend. Soon he began asking many things. Although his questions seemed random, there was an intent behind them. Soon, he gave voice to it.

# CHAPTER 26 –

## WHAT DO YOU BELIEVE

"My friend, I must ask you for a favor. Please, open the secret thing which you keep about your arm. Show me the magical armlet Nestan gave to you. Tell me about your love for this prize. Seeing the wonder of this thing again will allow me to rest my soul. Let me watch how the gold moves and tell me of your feelings for this thing."

Tariel unclasped the magical artifact. He then spoke of the thing with reverence, holding the golden circle out towards his friend.

"How can I tell you of such a thing? Nothing compares to Nestan, but this armlet she gave me is of incomparable beauty. It is all I have left from her hand. For me, this is the whole of my life and better than all the world. It is more precious than water, earth, or tree. You will find nothing like this anywhere else. Those who might say otherwise would be liars. Their words should not be listened to, for they would be more bitter than vinegar!"

With a sly smile, Avtandil refused to take the armlet. Instead, he took Tariel's wrists and pushed them back. He did not want to touch the armlet. He wanted to observe his friend's response. After a pause, he said as much.

"You have said exactly what I expected to hear. As they were your words, I will now share my thoughts. However, do not think I seek to flatter you. Rather, quite the opposite, for to lose Asmath would be far worse than losing this bauble. What you have is only gold, however much magic the item may possess. An alchemist or a goldsmith forged this wonder, but the thing is inanimate."

"You will find no life, speech, or reason therein. Yet you chose to die with this piece of metal and, in doing so, abandon a woman who has forever been your most ardent supporter. Truly I say to you, I cannot commend your behavior in this matter. This is a true judgment, for the poor maiden has been forever luckless."

"First, she grew up with and raised Nestan. She was the servant who first arranged your meeting. Then, unworthy of you, she gave herself up to your cause. In the end, her loss was that of a sister, but you have forgotten this."

"More, she came to you when Nestan was taken by the Kadjis, and you brought her with you. She is no less mad for your lover than you. Yet you chose to lay in the fields and die rather than return to her. She who trusts you above all else in this world. Can she survive without you, or should she die alone in the caves of the Devi?"

"You made a choice and, in doing so, have made it clear you no longer want Asmath. Yet she cries for you, even now, waiting and worrying over your fate. You are the only brother and family left to her, but you turned your back and abandoned her. Do you understand what a thing you have done?"

"This is not a vain or rash judgment. I speak the truth,

and you must not turn away from it. Information always has a cost, and you need to understand your actions for what they are. To anyone other than me, it might seem you no longer wanted Asmath. But I am closest to you, and I understand. Sometimes our hands and our head move counter to our heart."

"What I speak of now is between us and not fit for the ears of another. But I must know the truth of your heart. Are you still willing to fight, and in doing so choose to live? Can you pick yourself up from defeat, in the name of those you have sworn to protect? Do you remember what it means to be a warrior?"

"All men and women are born, and from them other things are birthed. Daughters, sons, revolutions, and wars. These are the things we all give life to, even into our own deaths. Because of this, there is no true difference between a man and a woman. They all fight to the end for survival, but only the strongest fight together. This was what you promised me, that we would fight together."

"Or have you forgotten your vows? Did you give up your sword for the robes and court attire of a petty Lord? Have you become a trader of lies and dishonesty, and chosen to take the path of a coward, forsaking what makes you a warrior? I hope not, but the words refuting this must come from you, for you need to understand what seeds you could so easily have sown in those who love you."

Tariel frowned as he listened to the words of his friend. He knew what he did was wrong and carried shame as his penance. What his friend said cut him deeply, but only the truest of knives bear deep wounds. Yet, he was also thankful for the boon of friendship. For only a true friend will tell another when he or she is wrong. He spoke shortly then, still newly returned to the land of the living and not having fully recovered his wits.

"What you say is true, though perhaps I would not

accept these words from any other. The fate of Asmath is indeed pitiable. She thinks forever of Nestan and sees only me. I thought of ending my life. This is what I have prayed endlessly for, as I receive no answer to my other prayers. But I still survive."

"You came in time to quench the fires which consumed my spirit and returned me to the road of men. Because of you I have lived to learn the mistake of my action. Let us return to her now, though you must forgive me in my hesitancy and shortness of speech. My mind but newly returned to the world, and still dazed with having nearly passed into the afterlife."

# CHAPTER 27 –

## IT CAN'T RAIN ALL THE TIME

Obedient to his friend, the two of them set out, intent on making their way back to the caves of the Devi. Tariel, the Amirbar, Grand General of India, was magnificent on his midnight steed, despite the wounds he bore. For his part, Avtandil shone like the star of Arabia. They were each beyond worth. Their teeth glistening like pearls as they spoke, words formed from lips made of cleft roses.

The wisdom shared by the Arabian could have filled the minds and books of sages. But there were still hidden designs behind what he said to his friend. For the sweetest tongues are those which lure serpents from their lairs. Avtandil knew this and spoke truths sharper than any dagger or sword.

"Brother, I will forever sacrifice mind, heart, and soul for your sake. But do not be as you are now and open your wounds anew with the passing of each day. You will find no end in this other than the destruction of all you love.

Yet you forever occupy this road to ruin."

"Each time I find you, there is a new peril with a tragedy of words and actions behind it. Have you no better way to spend your energies than this? What if we find Nestan tomorrow? In what state are you to rescue her? Your mind is spent, and your power depleted."

"Could you once more conquer the armies of Ramaz as you are now? Or would you fall beneath his sword, adding another tragedy to your burdens? Worse, gifting victory to the unworthy, and in the name of a tyrant? How would Nestan feel were such a thing to pass?"

"Learning will not help you if you do not listen to what the wise have said. Truly, I tell you, what advantage is all the hidden treasure in the world if you refuse to use it? Although a river may run deep, it is the waters which do not move fast which keep its course fixed. Still waters run deep. So should the soul of a Knight."

"Grieving will not bring you happiness, and therefore is of no use to you. No man dies without design, except by his own hand. Even without the sun, a rose may last more than three days. Why should you be different? Wait for your sun, though the night may be long. Work towards your victory. With luck and the grace of God, you will find what you seek. Despite the weather Fate may bring upon us, you must remember it cannot rain all the time."

When he heard what his friend said, Tariel was quiet. His thoughts turned inward. His sight, previously darkened by the veil between worlds, began to clear. He spoke with a degree of clarity and presence of mind for the first time, gifting Avtandil with the truth.

"Your words educate me, and this lesson is worth all the world. Once more, you have become a teacher to me, and the intelligent love their instructors, for what they say often pierce the hearts of the senseless. Thank you for taking the time to teach me. Without you, my own hand would have brought ruin upon all I love."

"Yet, I still do not know how I will endure this life when I have no end to my troubles. Better I should die with honor than survive in disgrace. For now, my grief has also captured your heart. I do not understand how you can justify remaining by my side. But I am thankful you are still a brother to me."

"I think it is because those who share afflictions are naturally drawn to each other. They have an affinity, like fire and wax. One feeds the other. In this way, you and I are matched. But your absence was like water to me, and if wax falls into water, the fire is quenched. The light dies, as I almost did."

"Both of us have been pierced by the lance of love, but you must understand the way my heart melts. I will tell you what happened while you were gone. When I am done, you may more clearly judge me with your wisdom. I only ask you to share the truth of your feelings with me when I finish telling you this story."

# CHAPTER 28 –

## LOVE BITES

"When you left for Arabia, I waited. However, the spring was long in coming, and I grew restless. Each day I roamed farther from these caves. I hoped for something to occupy my mind and hands, but I only grasped at straws. Hunting gave me no joy. With every new dawn, the caves became more prison than home."

"I longed for the wind and sun on my face but did not enjoy them without you. My failure to find Nestan pummeled my spirit each time I went out. In time I chose to ride on the plains, hoping the change of season would give me peace. But it did not. Every space was empty no matter what I did or where I went."

"For a time, I kept my gaze to the west for signs of your arrival. I rode far across these wild lands without any sign of you. Though you and I made vows to one another, loneliness and separation makes the best of men desperate. I became heartsick and lost, allowing this to make a fool of me."

"I rode farther and longer than I had before. My heart was not concerned for Asmath, as the Devi caves were well stocked with food, and she has water from the spring. Because of this, I did not fear for her safety. If I had feared for my own, perhaps I would be sharing a different story than the one I now relate to you."

"I came up the hill where you found my steed. From that place, I rode down and came into the reeds. Looking out across the marshes, I saw a lion and a panther together. I thought they were in love with one another. Seeing them like this brought joy to me, and I took it as a sign from God. A reminder to me of my love for Nestan."

"At first, they playfully ran to and from each other. It was a joyous chase, and they seemed like a picture of lovers. The sight of them quenched the burning fires in my heart, so I stopped to look as they played among themselves. But what they did next surprised and horrified me."

"They began to struggle against one another, fiercely quarreling over matters I did not understand. The panther fled, and the lion chased her. Each time they came together, they struck one another with their claws. In time she lost heart and fled from him, but he gave chase."

"Whatever she did, he would not be calm. He pounced on her, biting and clawing, and she fought back with a ferocity equal to his. Neither of them feared death, but they did not behave in a commendable manner. However, the lion was clearly overpowering her."

"I was not able to understand the behavior of the lion nor fathom his aggression towards her. Displeased with him, I shouted, asking why he so fiercely abused his beloved. Frustrated and angry, I drew my sword and rode towards him."

"My horse quickly closed the distance, and I struck the lion's head, breaking by blade as it struck his skull and killing him with a single blow. My sword freed him from the woes of this world, and I threw it down, leaping from my saddle as I did so. Reaching my hands out, I caught the wounded panther and tried to soothe her."

"For Nestan's memory, whose fires still burn my soul, I wished to kiss her. Yet she would not let me. She roared, maiming me with her claws and shedding my blood. Able to endure no more, I became angry with her abuse of me."

"With an enraged heart, I lifted her up and dashed her to the ground, shattering her body. She died in my arms. As I watched the life fade from her eyes, I remembered how I had quarreled with my own beloved. Looking around me at the ruin I brought on these poor creatures, my soul tore when I understood the horror of what I made myself a part of."

"Battered and beaten, I tried to crawl away from her corpse, disgrace and shame filling the void left in me as blood poured from my wounds. I fell where you found me. Though, to be honest, I wished for nothing more than to die where I lay. Can you not understand why I sought to cross into the next world?"

"The loss of Nestan has separated me from this life, yet death has become shy of me. These are the woes that grieve me. If I knew the road away from here, I would take it. But for me, every path seems to end in ruin. I fear no light can pierce the darkness of my existence."

"Now you know the reason for my absence. It was never my intention to abuse our vows. But even the best intentions can lead one to destroy what they love most. This is what happened to me, but I did not see it then. I am sorry and hope to find forgiveness and understanding in the warmth of your brotherly wisdom."

Avtandil embraced his friend, moved by the story of the lion and the panther. This was not the first time he had comforted his brother. Nor would it be the last. He understood the bitter wound branded across Tariel's heart better than anyone else in the world. The behavior of his friend did not surprise him, but he felt the need to make his forgiveness understood.

"Patience, my friend, is becoming of you. Do not die from the pain of your inadequacies. God will be merciful to you, but it is for Him to decide the when and where of His mercy. I know sorrow has been a constant companion to you, but Heaven would not have united you with Nestan if you were meant to be apart. However, these things take time. Acceptance and awareness do not happen according to any schedule other than the divine."

"A man's work in the fields does not bear fruit on the first day. Neither does a woman's womb produce a child at conception. You must be patient and carry this burden for yourself and your love. More, remember there is no lie in being who you are. But stop pretending to be something you are not to avail yourself of an easier road out."

"Mischance pursues the lover. This is the way it has always been. Those who follow their hearts always find bitterness in life, for love is grievous. It brings one near to death, maddening the learned and teaching the untaught. But those who bear this woe find that with time their suffering yields joy. Do you understand what I am telling you?"

Tariel nodded, indicating he understood, and Avtandil continued speaking.

# CHAPTER 29 –

## LITTLE THINGS

"There will always be those who have and those who have not. In life, we are one or the other, but never both. No one can have everything and keep themselves whole. Neither can he or she be whole without being able to accept the emptiness of loss and still embrace the joy of love."

"Those who would rise to enlightenment must bear the burden of knowledge, which is why all good men and women are cursed. It is only fools who are ever truly blessed, for their lives are free from obligation and debt. This is the way of the world, particularly for those like us who are Knights and men of the earth."

"Now, let us put grievances and hurts aside. You have no need to ask for forgiveness or understanding from me. Such baubles are the currency of strangers, and we are brothers. The time for talking has passed, and we must go. Asmath waits for us in the caves of the Devi."

The two brothers rode towards the caves at a slow and steady pace. One was injured, wounded of soul and mind. He looked like a sun tucked behind clouds. The other was bright as a shining moon and ready to give aid and support to his friend.

After some time, they came to the cliffs, and Asmath ran out to greet them. She wept tears of joy to see Tariel and busied herself with caring for his wounds. When she was satisfied with her salves and his numerous bandages, she asked how he had been so grievously wounded.

The two Knights then related the tale to her. First, Tariel spoke of what had happened. When he finished, Avtandil shared the details of how he found his friend and brother near to death. He spared no details, explaining how he guided the man back to the realm of the living from the edges of the underworld.

When Asmath heard the story, she could not contain her joy at Tariel's return to life. She praised the Almighty, blessing His grace and kindness. Her thanks were only outnumbered by the tears of happiness she cried while speaking.

"Oh God, whose majesty and grace cannot be expressed by man's tongue. You are the fullness of all and illuminate us with Your sunlike radiance. What can I say to give thanks to you, whom the intellect is unable to justly honor? Glory to You, who has not slain me with the shedding of tears over these two brothers!"

Both men bowed their heads when she offered her words of praise to the Heavens. They answered with their own silent prayers, for each had reasons together and of their own for showing gratitude.

Yet, more than anything else, they were thankful to be reunited. It was more than enough blessing for any of them. Yet, Tariel still carried a burden of guilt for his abandonment of Asmath, which he shared with her.

"Sister, my heart has bled often in these caves and on the fields. Fate makes us weep and smile in the same breath, but I would be remiss if I did not apologize for my behavior. I have seen a truth these days, though my eyes were blind to it before. Were it not for my love of you, death would be a joy. Yet I am in your debt for tears."

"Soldiers all knows a lack of water will slay them more surely than any blade. But what sane person would pour away the water of life when thirsty? I have often asked myself why the well of my sorrow has never dried. But it has filled the river of love between us. Without it, no rose would ever open, and the pearl of beauty would be lost. I understand this clearly now and will never again forget you or the radiance of your smile."

"You have forever been a sister to me and an advocate on my behalf, and our woes are united. So too are our victories. No more will I abandon you and take to roaming the wilds as I have done before. We will succeed or perish together. Though I am unsure how we will find Nestan, I cling to the hope we will succeed one day."

Tariel's words reminded Avtandil of Tinatin. She was his sun and beloved to him above all else. Though his vows kept them apart, he held close to his faith and devotion for her. Like water evaporated from the sea and returned to the mountains as rain, he knew he would one day find his way back home. Moved by the inspirational words of his friends, he voiced the song in his heart.

"Tinatin, my beloved. Life away from you has left me pitiable and unworthy of praise. I cannot tell you how I suffer or of the fires consuming my soul. Every day I ask how I will go on living without you, and each night I promise to answer myself in the morning. This way, I continue to do what I must, despite the pain of separation."

"Sometimes I wonder how a rose can convince itself

that when the sun sets, it will not wither and die without light. Yet the sun forever falls behind the world each day, reminding me it is better to harden my heart through the night. Perhaps I could petrify myself, so I no longer endured this hurt. But I would not deny myself the dream of returning to the warm and radiant touch of your love."

"Better I open my heart like a sail, so it might sooner carry me home to you. In this way, my spirit will not be spent. I will remain fresh of mind and body, so no task can defeat me or delay my return to you."

The three of them went on like this for some time, each praising the other or someone they loved. When night came, all of them went into the cave. Asmath stretched out Tariel's panther skin so they could sit together and rest comfortably. Each of the three spoke to one another of little things, calming the aches in their souls and hearts.

However, the men had not eaten in days. While Tariel rested, Avtandil prepared meat and Asmath made a fire for cooking. Pleasant conversation drifted between them as they waited for the wood to burn into coals for cooking.

# CHAPTER 30 –

## EVERY ROSE HAS ITS THORN

When the fire was ready, Avtandil began to roast meat over it. As is often the case amongst friends, their meal was a simple affair. They had neither guests nor bread, but hunger turns the most basic things into delicacies. Despite there being only meat and water, it seemed to Avtandil he had never tasted anything better.

Yet, Tariel could barely eat. Though he tried to chew a little food, he had no power. Despite the urging of Asmath, most of what he tried to swallow ended up being spit out. However, his spirits were much improved, and he wanted to talk with his friends.

Agreeable conversation is always pleasant. It comforts someone when they can speak of their troubles with a person who understands. A friend who will listen intently and not let what is said pass in vain. Such talk is enjoyable, and this was what he craved. It was what they all wanted.

The two Knights shared their difficulties and pains,

speaking late into the night. They revealed their woes and took turns offering advice and comfort to one another and with Asmath. Because of this, the fires which burned them were lessened.

When the sun rose, the two heroes stood and went out of the cave. They basked in the morning light, stretching like young lions before talking about the promises they made with each other. As they spoke, Asmath brought them a light breakfast. Tariel was finally able to eat, and once his hunger was satiated, he began speaking.

"I wonder why we share so many words between us. You have done so much for me, and God will surely repay you for your devotion. But between us, as men, oath for oath is enough. Remembrance of our vows and the friends we love are not the deeds of a drunken man."

"However, I must ask you to be merciful and kind with me as I tell you what is on my mind, for the furnace which burns me is not lit by any ordinary fire. It has not been kindled with steel but rather through the agony of my suffering. You have no ability to put out these flames. Even He who created me cannot free my soul from the fires."

"You are aware of this, for it is the reason I roam the fields like a madman. Though I was once a better man, this time has passed. Now, I cloak myself in madness, and reason runs from me like water off a duck's back. To save yourself from a similar fate, you must turn away from me and seek brotherhood elsewhere. If you do not go away, these flames will eventually consume you too, and I would not see your life extinguished as mine has been."

Avtandil was shocked to hear what Tariel said. His words were surprisingly compassionate and wise, but they were not something the Arabian could accept. The oaths of faithful men are stronger than steel. No fire can burn or blunt their edge. Moreover, no Knight ever abandoned his brother like a broken sword in the field.

"You surprise me with the depth of your words, yet I must question your cause in attempting to have me renounce my vows. How do you imagine I would leave you or think God was unable to cure your wounds? I am your sworn companion. More, His hand is responsible for everything planted or sown on this earth."

"Why would God create someone like you only to bring about your ruin? Surely, He will unite you once more with Nestan, though it is not for mortals to understand the time or place. Those will be of His choosing. We have no power to compel Him in this matter."

"Look deeper into your affairs my friend, and you will find the truth beneath your pain. Mischance pursues the lover. It has always been so, and it will always be. Every rose has its thorn. You are aware of this. If you and her never meet each other again, slay me as a traitor."

"Do you not ask yourself what it means to be a man? Though I am certain you know I will remind you. A man is one capable of enduring the most grievous of hurts. He stands tall and does not allow grief to bend or break his form."

"But a Knight must stand higher. He must be above other men and never forget the generosity of God, however difficult and hard the world may be towards him. This is a lesson I have no choice but to teach you again, and you must not forget it. I tell you, he who will not learn is more stupid than a donkey. Do not make yourself an excuse of a man, especially not before me."

"I asked my only sun, Tinatin, for her blessing to leave and come to you. I said to her, 'Tariel has made cinders of my heart. I cannot rest knowing my brother suffers alone. Because of this, I am no longer of use to you. I will not stay. What else is there to say?'"

"Yet, she did not turn her face away. Neither did she chastise me for my vows to you. Instead, she gave me sweet words, saying, 'I am content to remain here and wait for your return. The attention you give this Knight is also a service to me. I would not keep any man by my side who betrayed his word. What sort of husband or father would he make? Better I should grow old and become a spinster than waste my life with a treacherous and faithless liar. You are my Hero. Now, go and tend to the needs of your friend and brother.'"

"Can you not see how many people support you? Though it may only be me who lifts his sword, there are those behind me who lend strength to my arm. If not for them, perhaps I would not have the strength to do this. But I think this is nothing you do not already know. Remember your battle with Ramaz? How many men and women traveled in your camp, setting up tents and managing supplies or food? What might have become of you and your men without those who carried water and baked your bread?"

"You and I are no more or less than the sum of those who support us, and I am here for you. But I must ask, what do you think Tinatin would say to me if I returned to Arabia now? I will tell you. She would ask why I came home like a coward. There would be no praise from her. Nor would I be able to face myself if I abandoned you to the whims of Fate."

# CHAPTER 31 –

## LEAVE NO STONE UNTURNED

Agitated by the direction of conversation, Avtandil stood and began to pace. He had enough of talking and wishing. Now was the time for doing something. Too much time and too many moments had already passed by them, and he said as much to Tariel.

"I think we should stop such discussions. They are no means to an end. We must decide on a course of action. From there, we may discover the solution to our problem. If we do nothing, we are doomed to grow roots here and forever occupy this cave."

"You are a man who must manage a difficult deed. But to do this, you need to be reasonable. Yet a rose withered from lack of sun cannot provide for itself. In your current state, neither can you do what is required."

"Because of this, you are no longer of use to yourself. However, you can help me, for a brother must act brotherly. If you will allow me to carry your burden, you will serve us both and further the cause of your beloved."

"Your search for Nestan will now become my own. For a year and a day, I will travel to lands other than those you searched. Wherever you have been, I will not go. Yet in the new places I visit, I will be as vigilant as you were and leave no stone unturned."

"Perhaps you will rest your heart in the deep well of wisdom while I am gone or allow it to wander madly through a maze of dreams. These things do not concern my task, but what you do in my absence does matter. In this, I only ask you to strengthen yourself."

"This means you must do more than keep from being consumed by the flames of your heart. You will need to prepare mentally and physically. If you do not, the task of rescuing Nestan will fall to someone more capable. One who still has strength in his arms and wits in his head. I do not think this a shame you wish to carry, so fortify yourself while I am away."

"For my part, I will gather news from every place I travel. When the roses outside these caves bloom once more in abundance, you will know the time of my return is at hand. Perhaps I will find news, but maybe I will learn nothing. Only time will tell us this."

"Whatever I find, you must be prepared to leave these caves with me when I return. As of now, you are not of sound mind or body. Heal yourself, and when I return, we will face whatever comes together. From where we stand now, you and I will decide our next course of action."

"However, should I exceed my promised time to return, and these roses fade and fall, it means I have died. Should this come to pass, I only ask you to remember me and shed tears over the loss of a brother. But do not increase your grief. Instead, continue your search in honor of my sacrifice and remembrance of me."

"Now, I will go far from here and do not know whether

horse or ship may fail me. Your duty falls to me as my own. I have no idea what God will do to me, but I place my trust and faith in His hand. Though Fate may blow ill winds upon my road, Heaven will guide and protect me."

Tariel sighed, defeated by Avtandil's determination. He knew his friend was right and could not argue with his logic. With a resigned but cheerful smile, he agreed.

"I will not weary you further. Nor will I say too much. Besides, however long I might argue, I can see you will not listen to me. It is not for me to say whether you have the right of things or not."

"As the wisemen say, if a friend does not follow, you must follow him. Do whatever he wants, and in the end all things will come to light. Perhaps you will see what I have not or find what was hidden to my eyes. This is my hope for us all. Though, I will worry for you."

"To the best of my ability, I will do what you ask. With time you will learn the difficulty of my affairs, but all roads have come to the same end for me. Roaming will not change things. When you return, I will be here, no matter the madness which may torture me in your absence."

"Should you come back to find my days shortened by God, you must care for Asmath. Forever be brotherly to those in need and remember me each season when these roses bloom. This will be our bond."

With those words, they finished speaking. Each swore fresh vows on their promises. After clasping hands, they agreed on how they would make their next steps. Tariel would show Avtandil the way he had come to these fields and hills, for there were no roads leading to or from the caves of the Devi. For a time, the two would ride together.

But first, the Knights needed to hunt. They couldn't leave the caves empty of provisions, otherwise Asmath would have nothing to eat except for roots and berries. Once ready, they mounted their horses and rode off to hunt together.

When they returned from hunting, their meeting with Asmath was bittersweet. She did not want to be parted from either of them. For her, their departure would add grief to grief. But she did not waste time with sorrow. Instead, she busied herself caring for them.

This night would be the last time she could share the warmth of their friendship until Avtandil returned. In the morning, duty would separate their roads. Tariel would ride to the sea with him, and then return to her.

She was determined to make their last night a joyous occasion. They would eat and drink together, sharing their dreams and hopes for the future. When she woke, the sun would bring the light of Heaven down on them, and their journey would start with God's own blessing.

# CHAPTER 32 –

## THE SLAYER OF MAN

In the morning, Avtandil said goodbye to Asmath. He wiped her tears away and promised to return. Then she hugged both Knights, begging them to be safe. When she was done, they mounted their horses and started down the winding path away from the caves of the Devi.

As they reached the edge of the trees, she shouted after them. Her words echoed from the stones and hills, carried down to them as they left.

"Oh, my lions! The sun has burned and consumed you. Who has a tongue sufficient to lament the sorrows you must carry? My woe is eclipsed only by the suffering of your lives!"

The two men heard her words, but they did not stop or turn back. However, what she said made them grow a bit wild. Each wondered how one heart could live between lovers without the other, or what power might enable it to continue beating when separated from life itself. Parting from loved ones and long absences slay men and women equally. But those who do not know these things cannot understand the difficulty and pain of separation.

The Knights thought of these things as they rode into the distance. After weeks of riding, they passed into lands Avtandil had never seen before. They crossed new and strange countries, all empty of civilization. Until, at last, they came to the edge of a vast sea, stretching to the horizon's edge.

The waters were bright, with gentle waves lapping at the sandy shore. White birds flew overhead, calling out to one another as they dove into the sea to catch fish. It was beautiful, and they stopped to appreciate the landscape before riding on.

They went on like this for days, Tariel explaining how long he had ridden in his search for Nestan. Each time they passed a familiar landmark, he would point it out or give some story about the hope he once held as he traveled from this place or that. At night they would rest and continue their journey in the morning.

Eventually, they came to a place with outcroppings of rocks and high cliffs. This, Tariel explained, was as far as he was able to go and still be sure of Asmath's safety without him. From here, they must part ways. Both men dismounted and embraced. Avtandil hugged his friend, promising to return soon as he asked for directions.

"Now, you must tell me the way to Phridon, who gave you the magnificent black steed you ride. He, who is Lord and King of Mulghazanzar. I will start my search there, for perhaps some new information has come from the ship captains. Maybe he has heard of lands we have not yet seen. Show me where I must go to find him."

Tariel stared out over the sea, lost in memories of the white walled city and her King, Phridon. The man was both friend and brother to him. Over the years his thoughts had wandered there many times, but he never spoke of them.

"You must go towards the east and then to the south. Keep the shore of the water forever on your right, and you will find the city. How many months it will take, I cannot say. When I rode away from that haven of light, I did not travel directly or quickly. No doubt you will make better time than I did for myself when I left."

They spoke a bit more until Avtandil spotted a goat on the nearby cliffs. He readied his bow and brought the animal down. Then the two of them carried it back to the seaside and prepared a fire.

Soon, the animal was roasting, and they were busy making camp. When their task was finished, they rested, helping themselves to the meat. Side by side, they watched the sun sink into the farthest corner of the sea, sitting together until the moon rose.

At dawn, they woke and cheerfully greeted one another. Their words would have melted the hearts of anyone who heard. Yet no one was there to listen, save perhaps the beasts and birds. Each man understood the other must go his own way. Though time would separate their paths, it could not heal the wound of separation.

They embraced one more time and turned to go their separate ways. One went back the way they came, and the other forward to an uncertain fate. Each making their way along a roadless track. As the distance grew between them, one or both would look back and shout praises to the other. But before long, they were too far apart to see each other or hear what was said.

The two disappeared, like two moons slowly fading to nothing. The brightest light of Heaven would have frowned at their sorrow, but the day was cloudy, so the sun could not see them. Fate and the world are too often like this. Sometimes generous, and other times miserly.

# CHAPTER 33 –

## THE FEELINGS OF A STONE

Avtandil rode until the sun behind him was on the far edge of the western sky, but not yet set. As he rode, he bemoaned the plight they all found themselves in. He missed Tariel and worried how his friend would fare. Though the Indian was a strong man, his pain had left him flawed, like a chipped crystal goblet.

"Alas, oh cruel world. How do you not realize our pain? What sickness grips Fate that she whirls us to and from one tragedy to another. Is your habit to bring woe to those who love?"

"All who trust in you weep endlessly. Why have you uprooted me from everything and left this endless track before me. My only consolation is to know God does not abandon men as you do. This alone keeps my head high, for, within His grace, I cannot fall too far from the light."

"Still, the pain of my soul stirs once more. Blood flows from wounds I thought healed. I have left the woman who holds my heart, my friends, and all I love. The only joy I keep lies in knowing whatever happens, all of us will be reunited one day. Perhaps in this world or in Heaven. It matters not to me."

"But I must remember, not all men are equal. There are many differences between one and the next, and some are wanting of character. The ones I hold close are measured no differently than I. They are equal to me, for we keep back the dark and forever defend what is right."

Yet, despite the bold words he spoke, his thoughts soon turned back to Tinatin. How he longed to look on her raven hair as it twined about her neck, or to stare into the jet of her depthless eyes. He imagined the coral of her lips as she spoke, revealing her pearl-like teeth with each new word. In his mind, she whispered his name.

Thinking of her left him feeling like the world turned into a barren and empty wasteland. He was far from her embrace, leaving the strong shape of his form quivering in agony. The ruby of his heart changed color, matching his thoughts. Soon it became deep blue, like finely polished lapis lazuli.

Though her absence pained him, he did not allow negative thoughts to cloud his mind. He knew the ruin such thinking had caused in Tariel and did not want to invite a similar fate on himself. Instead, he called out to the fading sun as twilight approached. His voice echoed from the rocky cliffs to his left. Then the sound danced over the waters of the sea to his right.

"I am aware of the darkness which seeks to overcome me, but this is expected. Why should I wonder at the absence of light when even the sun has abandoned me? With this knowledge, my feet are sure and my steps righteous. Whatever brightness I may lack from without, my soul has an abundance within. I will not let any shadow darken what gives life to me."

"The sun and Tinatin are one and the same, for they are of equal radiance. Their light is mirrored by every planet I look on in the night sky, as the brightest stars shine with the glow of her reflection. In the day, she bears warmly upon me, and her light breathes life into all the world."

"She illuminates the mountains and valleys I travel over and through. Seeing her brings such joy to me I feel maddened by its intoxication. I never weary of basking in the warmth of her loving rays, but now I must ask where they have gone. At this moment I watch the light fading as my love drifts towards the world's edge. Soon she will sink into the water, and my heart will be cold again."

"Indeed, when the sun is far in winter, then we freeze for months. Yet now, I have been separated from her warmth for more than two months. How can any man's heart not be hurt by this? I am made from earth, not of it. This, I think, is the true source of my pain."

"Only a rock feels nothing and is never hurt. Stone has no understanding of life. But I live and breathe. I ache and sigh with the sharp pain of separation. Perhaps this is the lesson I must learn. A knife is not able to cure a wound, for it only cuts and causes swelling. Because of this, I must turn away from the blade of her absence. Instead, I need to focus on the light of the love she shines over me."

As he rode on, he considered how best to keep himself safe from the darkness of ill thoughts. Eventually, he decided to offer prayers to each of the brightest lights in Heaven. He would invite them to visit their judgment on him, carrying his words across the world to Tinatin.

# CHAPTER 34 –

## THE SEVEN GREAT LIGHTS OF HEAVEN

Avtandil stopped his horse and dismounted. He made a small camp and turned to face the sun as it dipped into the sea. Holding his arms out, he began his prayers by addressing the brightest light of Heaven.

"Sun, who is King of all, and mightiest of the mighty, I pray to you. Through your light, the humble are exalted. Give me happiness and sovereignty over myself. Do not keep me long separated from my beloved. I beg of you, do not turn my day into night."

Having spoken to the first of the Seven Great Lights, he sat at the edge of the waters and watched until sun dipped into the sea and was gone. With the last bit of twilight to guide him, he made a small meal but lit no fire. He would require darkness to be able to see the brightest lights in the night sky and did not want anything to dim their radiance.

Soon, the stars began to appear. When Avtandil was

satisfied at their number and the moon at last appeared, he sang for them in a high and sweet voice. He used their true names and spoke of Tinatin to each. In this way, he hoped his words would carry to the Heavens.

"Zual, Saturn, and planet of woe, I call you. Add tears upon my tears, and woe to woe. Dye my heart black and bind me in the thickness of gloom. Heap loads of grief on me as though I were a pack animal. But for her, I beg you to say, 'Do not forsake him. He is yours, and it is for you he weeps.'"

"Mushthar, Jupiter, and planet of justice, I seek judgment. You, who are the perfect judge, come and do justice. The heart takes counsel with heart, and I ask you not to twist justice. I am a righteous man. Why would you gift me with fresh wounds? Judge me, but do not destroy my soul."

"Marikh, Mars, and bringer of vengeance, do not show me mercy. Pierce me with your spear and stain my spirit red with the flow of blood. You know what I have become, for the path to joy in me is overgrown. Tell her of my sufferings. Let her hear them with your tongue."

"Aspiroz, Venus, who heals all, lend me your aid. Do not abandon me, maddened as I am from the effects of your power. She who encircles the pearls of her teeth with lips of coral has consumed me. I am lost to the flames of love. You who give such charm to the beautiful, do not leave me to ruin."

"Otarid, Mercury, wisest and planet of learning. Other than you, no other shares a fate like mine. Sit down to write the woes I endure. For ink, I will give you a lake of tears. Your pen, I will shape from my form, slim as a reed. Tell my story, for the sun whirls me to and from. It will not let me go and unites with me, burning away all I am."

"Come to me, great Moon, and take pity on my soul. I shrink with the passing of each day, wasting away to nothing. I am like you, filled by the sun yet emptied by it. Sometimes I am full-bodied, and other times there is nothing left of me. Tinatin is my sun, and I am her moon. For her sake, I die every day. Please, I beg of you, tell her who tortures me with her absence, 'Do not forsake him!'"

"This is my song, sung in prayer to the Seven Great Lights of Heaven. A million stars shine above me, and my testament is confirmed by these vows. Oh Sun, Otarid, Mushthar, and Zual, faint for my sake! Moon, Aspiroz, and Marikh come and bear witness. Give the woman who consumes me to understand the fires I suffer without her beside me."

"And to you, my heart, I must also sing. My tears still flow! They have not dried. Why do you slay yourself? I know who has maddened me, for she has hair darker than the tail feathers of a raven. But you, have you taken the Devil as your brother? Have you forgotten that without grief, the sweetness of joy can never be understood?"

"Life is uncertain, this much is true, but if I remain living, perhaps I will see my Tinatin again. In this way, I will be unburdened from sorrow. My soul will sing once more, and her who I love above all will stay by my side."

All the creatures of the forest came to listen as the words of Avtandil's song hung in the air. Even the stone cliffs marveled at the beauty of his voice. It was sweeter than the lullaby of a nightingale, and springs of sweet water erupted from the rocks, weeping fountains as he carried on singing into the night.

His words were the melody of all living things, and every creature on earth applauded him. Game from the forests, fish in the water, crocodiles in the sea, and birds from the sky. From every corner of the world, they praised him. Prayers even came from as far east as the endless ocean to the west beyond the Egyptian lands of Misrethi.

# CHAPTER 35 –

## Don't Talk to Strangers

In the morning, Avtandil stood and greeted the sun as it lit the world around him. The sky was rose and gold, which he took to be a good omen. With a light heart, he ate breakfast and resumed his ride towards the distant lands of Mulghazanzar.

For seventy days he kept his course, never pausing or stopping for more than rest. He hunted as he rode, ever mindful of the single year he had been given to learn of Nestan and return to Tariel. He always stayed near the sea, and on the seventieth day, he noticed a ship at anchor. Sailors were rowing to the beach and would land not far from where he was.

When they arrived, he rode up to them, asking who they were and what lands he was in. Surprised to find a lone Knight on the edges of the water, the men removed their hats before answering. With respect towards his status as a Lord, they answered.

"Greetings, fair Knight. It is most pleasant to meet one such as you, so fair of form and fluid in speech. You stand now on the farthest edge of the lands of Turkey. Further to the east is our realm. With pride, we will tell you about our Lord."

"His name is Nuradin Phridon, and he is King of these lands. He is brave and mighty. His generosity knows no equal among the people, and to those in need, he is ever kind. None in our lands can compare to him, and his beams spread over us like the light of Heaven."

When he heard their words and the name of Phridon, Avtandil's smile shone brighter than the sun. He could not believe his fortune to have met men of the lands he hoped to find. His joy knew no bounds at hearing he had nearly reached his destination.

"Brothers, it is my luck to have met such men as you. I seek your King and bear pleasant tidings for him. Please, show me which way I must go. And tell me, is it far?"

Though the sailors had other tasks, they stopped their work and guided him a bit farther up the beach to a small hill. From their vantage, the men pointed to a distant road. They explained where Avtandil should go.

"That is the road to Mulghazanzar, which is our city. Within the walls of the Kingdom, you will find the palace of our King, he of the swift arrow and keen sword. To get there, you must ride for ten days."

"But before you leave, please tell us who you are. We have not seen another man like you. You are formed like a tall cypress, and your cheeks shine like rubies. Why do you, a stranger to us, consume our hearts like fire when we look on the grace of your form?"

Surprised at their devotion towards him, Avtandil explained who he was. But he did not tell them the purpose of his journey or why he was traveling. These were not men who needed such details. It was better to be cautious with strangers, however kind or adoring they might be.

"I am Avtandil, a Knight from the far lands of Arabia. Though, I must confess my surprise at your adoration of me. I could agree if you witnessed me when the rose of my heart was not so faded. In those times, I was proud and not crippled by separation from my beloved. In those times, the men and women who sat with me were charmed. But now I am a shadow, though your praise is a welcome joy to my day. Thank you."

They exchanged more pleasantries and then shared a meal together. Avtandil provided meat from what he had hunted while the sailors offered bread, wine, and cheese. Their meeting was a sign of good things to come, making for an excellent start to the day, and they were all pleased.

When they finished eating, the sailors returned to their ship. The Knight watched as they left, and then turned away from the water and headed towards Mulghazanzar. He had ten days to travel but hoped to make less of it by riding quickly.

When he reached the road, he put his horse to a canter relaxing as he rode. At various points along his journey, he passed many different people. They all bowed to him. Many were in awe of this beautiful stranger in their lands and offered him small gifts and pleasant conversation.

But he had no time to spend with them. Instead, he confirmed the directions and time to his destination from each person he met. As the days passed and he grew closer, more and more people could be found on the roads. Before long, he began ride through small villages and understood he would soon reach the end of his long road.

On the last day of his journey, towards the afternoon, he saw Mulghazanzar on the far horizon. But the plain between him and the city was swarming with soldiers hunting game. They had ringed the field, and beaters chased out bird and beast alike. Whatever came out was mowed down by the hunters like corn beneath a scythe.

Drawing closer to them, Avtandil spotted a young man standing a bit separated from the rest. Pulling him aside, he asked about the host of soldiers and hunters on the fields. The youth told him it was the custom of Lord Phridon, King of Mulghazanzar, to sometimes hunt and sport on the plains with his soldiers.

Avtandil thanked him for the information, and then rode towards the troops with his head held high. He was full of joy, knowing the first part of his journey was nearly over. Looking up, he watched as an eagle soared overhead. Emboldened by the sight, he urged his horse forward and drew his bow.

The soldiers he passed were held in thrall at the sight of his graceful form. They stood in awe as he let a single arrow fly, bringing down the eagle with one shot. It fell, blood flowing, and the Knight dismounted. In front of all the gathered soldiers, he clipped its wings, and then calmly mounted his horse again.

From all sides, Phridon's men came towards him, but he kept riding forward with a slow and deliberate pace. The men were so in awe of him they dared not ask who he was. Archers stopped shooting, standing with their mouths agape, but none had words or power to present him with the bouquet of speech.

Yet he did not stop or slow his horse. He had been noticed by a mounted Knight on a hill at the far side of the meadow. This man did not look pleased to see Avtandil.

# CHAPTER 36 –

## TWIN SUNS

Avtandil counted forty men standing around the Knight on the far hill. Each one held a bow, and to be standing where they were, they must have been worthy of shooting with their Lord. He was sure the man standing above them must be Phridon, and this was the direction he continued in. The hunters and soldiers from the fields followed behind him, unable to do anything other than stare in awe.

For his part, Phridon had noticed the foreign Knight approaching and watched as his troops followed the man like lost sheep. He could not understand what his armies were doing or why they wandered as if in a daze. It angered him to see such a lack of discipline, and he ordered a servant to find out why they had stopped hunting and were stumbling about like blind men.

However, when the servant reached the soldiers, he too lost his tongue. The sight of the stranger left him unable to speak. All the words he had been told to say fled from his mind. But Avtandil understood why the man came and spoke to him.

"Good man! I beg you, please deliver a message from me to your Lord on the hill. Tell him I am a stranger, far removed from my home, and have spent nearly three months reaching this place. Though I am weary, loneliness gnaws at my belly with greater urgency than any hunger. I have been sent by Tariel, my sworn brother, and wish to speak with the King of these lands."

The servant bowed, unsure of what else to do, and returned to Phridon. However, he had become too enamored of the strange Knight and was uncertain of what was supposed to say.

"Lord, the man below us seeks to converse with you. He is like a sun and lightens the day to all who lay eyes upon him. As I speak to you now, I cannot clearly recall what he said, for even sages would be maddened if they looked too long on him. Yet he told me he has come from afar to see you. More, he said his brother is Tariel."

When he heard the name, Phridon jerked his head up with a start. He did not believe his ears, hearing of Tariel after so long with no word or whisper from the man. At once, his woe over his friend's absence lessened, though his worry did not diminish. His heart became agitated, for perhaps this stranger brought ill news. But at the same time, he was curious. He wondered who this man was to hold his armies in thrall and cause the tongue of his messenger to fail.

He hastily rode to meet Avtandil, concern etched on his face and hope flying in his spirit. Torn between joy and sadness, he kept himself composed. The blast of emotions he experienced froze a measure of his soul, and snowstorms of tears whirled behind his eyes, waiting to frost his black lashes. Yet he clung to hope of good news.

When he reached the stranger, the two men dismounted and appraised one another. They were like twin stars staring across the Heavens, or the moon reflected at itself from a twilight pool. Though strangers to each other, they were not shy. When Avtandil said Tariel was well and sent his regards, Phridon grabbed him in a joyous embrace, and they hugged like lost brothers.

Eager to talk in private, Phridon beckoned Avtandil towards Mulghazanzar. They mounted their horses and rode off together. The awestruck soldiers and hunters following behind. As they rode, Avtandil began to speak.

"No doubt you are eager to learn more of me. When we sit, I will tell you everything you wish to know. Where I have come from, and how I came to be called a brother of Tariel. He has already told me much of your story, but I would also hear it from you."

"Like you, I seek to aid his cause. Hopefully, we can find news of Nestan where before he was unable to. The grief of her loss does not blind my eyes so much as it does with him. By the grace of God and with luck, perhaps I will discover a light where he found only darkness."

# CHAPTER 37 -

## A HISTORY OF VIOLENCE

After a short ride the two Knights arrived near the walls of Mulghazanzar. The guards watching the gates cheered as their King rode into the city, and people stopped to stare when they saw the beautiful stranger beside him. This adoration continued as the two men rode towards the palace, where groomsmen took their horses.

Soon, the Knights were sitting together in the gardens overlooking the sea. They snacked on fresh fruits and sipped hot mint tea while waiting for servants to bring food. Able to finally rest, Avtandil began telling Phridon of himself and his tale, speaking intently and in detail.

"I am a Knight serving King Rostevan, Lord of Arabia. In my lands, I am the Grand Commander in Chief of the armies and called Avtandil by my people. My name comes from a noble house, but I grew up as an orphan. Battle took my father before I was born, and my mother was lost to the difficulties of bringing me into the world."

"However, the King was like a brother to my father, so he raised me up as his own son. I grew well under the tutelage of such a powerful man. Because of this, our people respect my skill in battle and presence of mind. But I am also a lover of the arts and philosophy."

"It came to pass that one day the King and I had a friendly wager between us to see who the better archer was. We roamed over the plains together, killing all kinds of wild beasts. When we finished, one of my men noticed Tariel sitting some distance away, though we did not have any idea who he was."

"Curious about who this beautiful and foreign stranger was and why he wept endlessly, we called out, but he did not answer. How could we have known of the fires which consumed him? Who might have guessed at how much pain the man carried branded across his heart? We did not know, and so Rostevan grew angry when Tariel ignored us. The King ordered soldiers to seize the stranger."

"Yet every man who approached him met a bloody and savage end. Those few who survived his blows were left with broken arms and legs, but they were the lucky ones. The other soldiers soon learned the chariot of the sun cannot be turned back by mortal men. Tariel educated them by making a pile of corpses from their ranks, slaying one after the other."

"The King, a Hero in his own right, became enraged. Realizing his troops were no match for this stranger, he and I took up arms. We mounted and rode towards Tariel, set on overcoming him together."

"Yet, he realized the King rode against him. When we approached, he looked directly at us. Then he slapped his horse and vanished before our eyes. Despite our best huntsmen trying to track where he went, we found no trace of his passing. It was as if some demon from the otherworld had come before us, or so we thought."

"After this, a deep and lasting melancholy consumed the King. His mood was black and full of sorrow for an entire year. In this time, we sent men from one corner of our Kingdom to the other. Still, none came back with any news of the Knight. When the last messenger returned with no new information, the King's spirit lightened, and he returned to joy."

"He decided the stranger was not human, for no man can vanish like that. This meant he had been a Devi, and there was nothing our soldiers could have done against such a creature. Few weapons can harm those things, for they are of the old race."

"However, his daughter Tinatin did not believe this. She was overcome with sorrow at the thought we had misunderstood the intentions of a valiant Knight, and now were set to abandon him to Fate. Her heart could not rest easy with the idea of leaving him alone to overcome whatever he was so deeply pained by. One night she summoned me and shared these thoughts."

"Though it is another story, we confessed our love for one another. She agreed to marry me, but requested I perform a difficult task first. I needed to spend three years alone, roaming the wilds in search of information about the mysterious Knight."

"At her behest, I stole away from Arabia to find him. The fires of love burned me with every step, and my heart smoldered in the absence of my beloved. But I searched everywhere for word or sign of him. Many are the nights I did not sleep. Such was my dedication to the quest set before me. Yet I found no sign or word of the man until the time allotted to my quest was nearly spent."

"Finally, on the far edges of a beautiful field of wild red tulips, I came across three Kurdish brothers. One of them was grievously wounded and near death. They told me of their story, and then pointed to the horizon. There, I saw the black silhouette of a man and horse fading into the setting sun. I knew it was the man I sought and hastily made my way towards him."

"Like the moon chasing the sun, I shadowed his every step for three days. I did not approach him out of concern he might disappear again or was indeed a Devi. In all those days, he never stopped to rest. Neither did I, for fear I might lose sight of him."

"At last, he rode up to some cliffs, and I observed the strangest of sights there. A black-haired and tear-stricken maiden greeted him. Together they sobbed and shared their woe over an issue I did not understand. When this finished, they went into the caves and did not come out again before the next morning. This was when the strange Knight rode away once more."

# CHAPTER 38 –

## THE BETTER PART OF VALOR

"Knowing I would not be able to easily approach him without bloodshed, I waited until he left. Then, I surprised the maiden and took her by force. I hoped she would tell me about him, but she denied my request. However, she was wiser than I and sisterly towards me. You know her, for she is Asmath, worthy of Kings and Kingdoms for her devotion and kindness."

"It was she who took me into the caves and told me some little of Tariel. Likewise, when he returned, her hand brought us together. Because of her, he welcomed me as a brother and told me all his story."

"Those caves once belonged to three Devi. They killed the other two Knights who came with Tariel when he first arrived there, though I never learned their names. Now, only Asmath remains from those who left Mulghazanzar. She attends to him and helps keep the fires of his anguish from destroying what remains of his spirit. But it is no life for either of them."

"He roams and hunts, feeding her like a lion feeds its cubs, but he does not go far from there. Besides Asmath, he has shut himself away from the race of men and only keeps the company of wild beasts. Until I heard of you, I thought he had no other man in the world than me as a companion. I cannot tell you how it brought joy to my heart to learn you are also a brother to Tariel. Between us, perhaps he is not so lost as I once feared."

"Not long after Tariel told me his tale, we made a vow of brotherhood to aid one another, no matter the circumstance. Our oath meant I must return to Arabia and relate his story to my beloved Tinatin. Then, once the fires in her heart had been quenched, I would come back to him so we might search for Nestan together."

"As promised, I returned home and shared the story of Tariel with my King and his Lords. Their hearts were deeply stricken when they heard of the woe he suffered. Later, and in private, I came to Tinatin and told her of my vows to help find Nestan. She agreed, accepting my own oaths as a service to her, and insisting I leave immediately to help my brother."

"However, Rostevan would not give me leave to depart. It was a great sorrow and burden upon my conscience. He unknowingly forced me to choose between betrayal of my Kingdom or my word as a Knight. But ultimately, I chose the better part of valor, keeping my promises unbroken. Instead, I dedicated them to the honor of my King."

"To assure Rostevan of my love for him and loyalty to our Kingdom, I wrote a letter. When I finished, I appointed my childhood friend and brother Shermadin to watch over the armies as I stole away in the early hours of the morning. Without stopping for anything other than rest, I hastily rode back to Tariel. But when I arrived, he was gone. I could not find him anywhere."

"Asmath had not heard from him for more than one week. I searched the plains near the caves, but he was not there either. Before long, I found myself roaming more distant places, though I learned nothing for days. When I had almost given up hope, I finally came upon him. His spirit was across the threshold of this life and nearly into the next. Death had taken him so far into the shadow realm that only a flicker of life remained in him."

"Through much coaxing and an endless stream of words, I managed to bring him back to life. However, he is not the man he was when you met him. His spirit is more damaged than anyone I have seen still living."

"He suffers more with each passing day. Like a lost sun, he endlessly roams over the same paths and trails, riding the black steed you gave him. But this is not what he wants. Instead, he longs to be cradled by the earth. He believes death is his only hope. Though I like to think my words and promises renewed his taste for life, I cannot say how long he will remain with us in the world of men."

"Now, I seek a balm for his soul. The fires of his pain consume him and all he touches. Without aid, he is lost, and with him, Asmath. I promised to go in search of Nestan for a year and a day. My return to him must be at the time when the roses around the mouth of the Devi cave bloom again. Until then, my route is to seek news of her by land and sea, down any road it takes me."

"This is how I came to find you. When I left the caves, I made a bittersweet farewell to Asmath. She asked me to tell you the stars still shine, and all is well. More, she gave me this ring as a gift for you. Tariel also sends his regards, though he could not leave Asmath alone. Instead, he left the caves to show me the way here."

"He and I rode together for many days until our ways parted. Without his help, I would not have known how to find you or the roads which brought me here. Though it has taken nearly three months, I am in your court. My thanks are with God and the Heavens for our meeting."

"However, I must ask about your conversations with Tariel. Is there some story of how you came to know one another which he did not tell me? Was there something he might have said or did, which perhaps can offer us a clue as to where Nestan might be? Have you heard anything of her since Tariel was last here?"

"More, are you aware of any places he has not searched for his beloved? With all the ships coming and going from Mulghazanzar, you must have learned many new things from distant ports. If you do not know something which can help us, is there someone other than you who might have such knowledge? Perhaps if we widen our nets, the catch will be worthy, and we may yet find her."

# CHAPTER 39 –

## THE ARM OF THE SEA KING

Phridon stared intently at Avtandil, considering everything the Knight said. His thoughts roamed back over the years, and he thought of all he did to help Tariel. In particular, he thought of how the seven years of their separation had brought him news of many far places. Though, he was not sure which information might help them most.

"You are aware of what happened between Tariel and me, and I have nothing extra to tell of my time with him. Though, one of his Knights did leave a journal with my scholars. Perhaps we will find some knowledge on its pages which we have not previously considered. But other than this, I cannot tell you anything you do not already know."

"However, we have learned of many new and distant lands since he left. I think we must discuss this, for you have the right idea of things. Perhaps by working together, we can find Nestan, the joy of all who gaze on her. She who disturbs those who cannot stare at the radiant sun of her being. Even I cannot forget her, though it was only the briefest of moments when my gaze rested on her beauty."

"You already know of the island Kingdom I wrested from the grasp of my treacherous relatives, yet it has grown tremendously over the years. Now we trade a hundred times what we did in those days. Ships sail our waters in abundance. The likes of which were only seen before from the greatest of Kingdoms."

"Chief among all the ships which visit our ports are those from the Sea Realm. Melik Surkhavi rules there, and he is known to all as the Sea King. Although perhaps you are not well versed in matters of the sea or he who rules it, so I will tell you what men of the land rarely understand."

"On the waters, honest men only use two coins for their trade. These are duty and fear. Duty because none dare contest the captain of a ship. He or she holds knowledge the crew lacks. So, they must observe their duties. Otherwise, they risk the embrace of a watery grave where none will remember their name or sing their praises in the afterlife."

"Fear is the other coin. This is because fear is the only thing other than duty more constant to sailors. On the sea, a man's fears take many shapes. Sometimes it is a storm or a wave of titanic proportions. Other times it's the loss of ships and men who are never seen again. But more than these things, it is the black sails of a pirate ship."

"Of pirates, though, they are a different and dishonest breed. They have a different set of fears, but there are three things they are afraid of. The least of those things is capture, which almost always ends in the loss of their lives. Death doesn't concern them because all sea men risk their lives equally every time they venture into the endless waters of the deep. So, pirates only fear death a little. Second among their fears is the Pirate King, though none have ever seen him or can say who he is. Some have even said it may be a woman, but all agree there is only one person more ruthless to those who cross him."

"That person is the Sea King. No one dares to cross him, and his arm extends up the entire eastern coast of Africa. He is chief among all things a pirate fears and many merchant ships pay a heavy toll to fly the flag of his kingdom on their vessels. For doing so ensures no pirate will disturb them."

"However, Melik Surkhavi is a private man. Though his Kingdom is said to be hospitable, he does not lightly entertain those who are strangers to him. I've even heard rumors whispered of him being the Pirate King. However, the words of any sailor must always be taken with a measure of salt. Such men also tell fantastic tales of giant sea monsters and islands of women warriors on the other side of the world."

"How much of their stories are true is any man's guess. But there is always a grain of truth in every lie. So, if you seek news in the Sea Realm, be cautious and vigilant of those around you when and where you go. Now, let us summon my scholars and see this journal Tariel's Knight left behind. We will soon know if anything of interest is written therein."

# CHAPTER 40 –

## LEGACY OF THE TWINS

B efore long, scholars arrived with the journal. It was worn, apparently from years of use, and bound in old, faded leather. As Avtandil began reading the faded pages, he was surprised to understand how well-educated Tariel's Knights had been.

Their names were Abu and Ardaz, and they were twins but not from India. They wrote of journeys and travels across different lands, describing many cities and regions wholly unfamiliar to Avtandil. Moreover, their notes contained records of places the two had not visited but which they kept notes of.

Chief among the unvisited places they wrote of was a fabled city. It was said to be seven days journey from the barren lands surrounding the fortress of Kadjeti. Somewhere on the eastern coast of Africa. They described it as fairer than a fresh pearl and named it Gulansharo. This, Avtandil felt, was the road he must take. His heart told him there must be news of some sort in such a place, but he was not well versed in Kadjeti or what it meant to be a Kadj. Curious, he asked about them.

He and Phridon discussed what they each had heard of the lands of Kadjis. It was not somewhere a man wanted to find himself by accident. The black-skinned Kadj sorcerers who lived there were betrayers of men. Their people engaged in slavery, piracy, and worse. Though not all were evil, theirs was a Kingdom of dark magics. The two Knights agreed it would be well to avoid their realm entirely. Though they had no solid information on the Kingdom, it was certain death was the only currency that place traded with.

Ship captains were summoned to discuss how Avtandil might make the journey to Gulansharo. But none of them could say exactly where the city was or how to reach it. The only information they had was from tales. The name was ancient and possibly no longer in use, so none could say exactly where or what it was.

For this reason, it was decided travel by land would be the best option. Phridon would send four of his best Knights with Avtandil. The five of them would leave Mulghazanzar in three days to begin their search.

Their course decided, they held a feast that evening. Although absent, Tariel was the guest of honor. Soldiers wept at the tragedies the King of India was forced to suffer. Some shouted praises to him, while others lamented and tore at their faces and hair. Phridon himself wept, speaking against the inconsistency and falsity of the vain world we lived in.

"Oh, my friend and brother! Since your departure, I have worn a rut through my soul with worry over your fate. Though you have not been able to return, my days have been filled with longing for you. I am oppressed by your absence. A measure of my every joy is taken from me until the day I might see you again. Life is empty without you. The world sometimes becomes hateful to me, for I cannot understand why you are so abandoned by Fate!"

Everyone at the celebration raised their glasses or voices to Tariel, their fallen Hero. They ate and drank in honor of him, filling themselves to their satisfaction. Then they did it again until everyone was over full of drink and food, and the talk turned towards Avtandil.

The gathered folk applauded him. Each was sure of the Lordship of the Arabian and said as much. They spoke of his heroism, devotion to Tariel, and attention to Phridon. Many there gave themselves over to the flames of affection with their love of the youth.

Over the following days, people from every part of the city came to the castle and gave gifts to Avtandil. Some gave silk, while others gave fine leather crafts and lovely jeweled rings and trinkets. In the end, it was more than he could carry, but he could not ignore their adoration. One who holds a position of leadership must always be aware of those he or she serves. And in turn, be mindful of those who provide service.

In their time between visits from the adoring hosts of Phridon, the two Lords hunted together. They did this each afternoon until the last day when they held a great hunt. From far and near, they slew whatever matter of game offered itself up to them. The archery of Avtandil put every bowman to shame, and many praised his skill. In time, he turned to the King of Mulghazanzar and voiced his thoughts.

"Parting from you is painful. I feel I harm myself in doing so. It is as if I court death and would abandon the joy of my life in your Kingdom. Yet, I do not have leisure to tarry here. The urgency of responsibility weighs upon me, and an unknown road yawns before me like a chasm. I would not be late in accomplishing my duties."

"Those who shed tears at separation from you are right in the deed, but today, without fail, I must leave. Waiting too long in one place is the mistake of an inexperienced traveler. Those who roam far would do well to remind themselves of this. Besides, you know of the fire which consumes me, and why I cannot wait. I beg of you, lead me to the sea, where you first saw Nestan. That is the place I will go from."

Phridon understood his friend could not stay, smiling as he told him not to worry. There would be no delay, for neither Tariel nor Nestan should suffer on behalf of those who still enjoyed their freedom.

"My friend, there is nothing I would say to hinder you. There is little time left and you must go to complete a duty only you are capable of. While it is true a lance pierces me when I think of your departure, I am comforted knowing God will guide you. Though it will be difficult to bear your absence, my every blessing goes with you."

With those words, Phridon led the Arabian towards the place where the two brutish Kadj kidnappers had arrived on their fantastic ship. Behind them, a hundred soldiers and more followed. Before long, they arrived at the cove where the glowing vessel had landed.

Knowing Avtandil would leave soon, the soldiers lamented their guest's imminent departure. Some saying winter would never freeze them again if only he would remain near as their sun. Others said they would close their eyes when he left, for the light of their lives would forever be removed from them. But Avtandil would accept no delay, however much he wanted to remain.

The needs of Nestan were greater than those of anyone there or elsewhere.

# CHAPTER 41 –

## MAHMAD'S FAITHFUL

Avtandil thanked his friend for guiding him there, remarking that the place was every bit as beautiful as Tariel had described it. Then Phridon turned towards the bay, speaking as he did so.

"It is here where the ruby-lipped moon you seek stepped forth from the strange glowing Kadj ship. Though I might have spirited her away from them with the strength of my sword arm, there was no way I could reach them fast enough. They fled like a bird on their ship. I was unable to give chase. Now, once more from this place, another moon departs me, and you will be sorely missed, my friend."

But this is the way of the world. Friends must part. Though they may pass their time together like two rivers winding through a valley, they cannot slow the sun's course through the sky by words or any other means. Everyone understood the truth of this, and so the two Lords embraced one last time. When they finished,

Avtandil turned and rode away. The four Knights followed, leading a sturdy pack mule, laden with provisions and gold.

Phridon and his soldiers watched as their Hero left. A sorrow gripped the men, as though some great tragedy passed over their hearts. Yet, every man and woman there was also aware of the weight of their own vows and oaths. They could no more forsake their duties than a King was able to abandon his people. Like Tariel before him, Avtandil made his way away from Mulghazanzar and into the wilds.

He and the four Knights rode west for almost a hundred days. Whenever they met travelers on the shore or nearby hills, they would ask for news of Nestan or the Kadj men who had taken her. But they found no one who knew anything. In time the setting sun became their compass, thought it didn't matter to Avtandil if it never set.

As the days passed with no news, the world became like straw to him. His spirit waned like the moon, and he cursed Fate for the burden of his loneliness and separation from Tinatin. Yet, thoughts of her also renewed his determination and gladdened his heart.

"Why does it forever seem I am burned by the devotion and sacrifice required of a Hero? How I long to be a normal man. I would spend my time by your side, basking in the glory of your sunlit form. Though I am far from you, the memory of your hand in mine brings joy to me."

"But woe to the ruin so freely sowed by the hand of Fate! You who are false, and at times a poison to the world. Though your actions seek to turn my heart to stone, I will endure. The balm of my soul lies in Arabia and awaits my return. Your evil hand will not long keep me separated from her pearl teeth and raven hair."

He held these thoughts high in his mind each day, until

one morning he and his Knights came across a merchant caravan. A long train of camels stood nearby, but the merchants were not moving. Instead, they were gathered at the edge of the water. Something had greatly disturbed them, but Avtandil could not understand what it was.

Curious, he approached and asked why they were so distressed. One merchant, apparently the leader, turned and answered.

"Oh, the sun before me! You are a vision of life and looking at you is a comfort to my soul. Come and sit beside us. I will tell you of the tragedy we are gripped by, for it is not a thing we have been able to remedy."

"My name is Usam, and I am the chief of this caravan. We are merchants who come from the distant city of Baghdad. Our faith is of Mahmad, and so we are not given to drink new wines. Yet we have heard of fine wines in the realm of the Sea King, so we have come from afar to trade. Our goods are of the finest quality, and we are certain of a handsome profit."

"Yet, as we arrived at this place, we found a man washed up from the sea. He was senseless and unable to speak coherently. A fever gripped him, and we feared he might die. At times he would shout out, gripped by some fear only he could see, saying strange things, such as, 'If you go in, they will slay you!'"

"In time, our healer coaxed him back to life. He roused, telling us of his plight. He said he'd come from Egypt with a caravan laden with many goods. Yet, when they found a merchant vessel and took to the seas, pirates attacked."

"He told us, 'They flew a black flag and sailed a ship fitted with an iron tipped ram. When they saw us, they crashed into us and killed everyone around me. All was lost, and though I thought myself to have died, it seems I still live. Yet, I do not know how I came to be on these shores.'"

"This is the cause of our worry and woe. For, what are we to do? If we return to Baghdad, our losses will be a hundred times the cost of our goods. But if we venture across the water as this man did, we will surely be slain by pirates."

"We are only humble traders, and none of us has the strength to fight bandits and pirates. This inability to protect ourselves leaves us trapped here. We cannot stay or go forward. Now you know the reason for our dismay."

Avtandil listened intently, taking in the measure of Usam as he spoke. He considered what the man said as he looked at the other members of the caravan gathered before him. Then, an idea came into his mind, though he said nothing of it at the time. Instead, he offered his aid and protection.

"You have the measure of honest and faithful men about you, but whatever comes from above cannot be avoided. Those who let grief overwhelm themselves become nothing, so their efforts are in vain. Do not be like this. You do your part as merchants, and I will take the surety of your blood upon myself."

"Whoever fights you will find themselves worn out by the point of my sword. My four Knights and I will accompany you. Together we will make our way to the next city and secure a ship. Fear not."

The merchants were overcome with joy at his words. They bowed in thanks, kissing his feet and offering their service to him. Yet he made them rise, saying that if he should require some assistance from them later, they could discuss it then. For the moment, he had no need and only sought to protect the innocent from harm.

They agreed to aid him in whatever way they could. He had only to ask. With their service promised later, the Knights and the caravan made their road towards the city.

# CHAPTER 42 –

## THE LONG TONGUE OF A BLACK FLAG

For two days, they journeyed towards the nearby city the merchants had mentioned. Two Knights rode before and two behind. Avtandil sat with Usam. They talked of the many places the traders had traveled. The Arabian wanted to know whether they knew of two black Kadj men and a woman like a moon come to earth. But no one had any information.

When they arrived in the city, it was a simple matter to book passage on a cargo vessel. The ship's captain was pleased five Knights would be joining them. He thanked God for their protection and soon the goods were loaded, and everyone was aboard. As the tide went out, they set sail across the sea.

Fair winds blew, and they made good time, heading west and occasionally south. The merchants discussed which port might best serve them and decided to stop first at a verdant city they had heard of. The merchant chief there was a man named Usen, whom they had heard of. He was said to be fair and honest in his dealings.

Things were peaceful over the next two days as they sailed towards their destination, but Fate reared her ugly head on the third day. Clouds darkened the sky, and a huge ship with the long black flag of the Pirate King approached from the west. It was heading right at them. Seeing no way to avoid it, Avtandil ordered his Knights to prepare themselves for battle.

As the ship closed in, he saw a long iron-tipped wooden beam jutting out from the prow. This was the same vessel Usam had described, but Avtandil was not worried. He took a heavy wooden club in his hands and stood at the edge of the deck as the enemy drew closer.

Across the glassy sea surface, shouts and trumpets of war echoed towards them from the pirates. The traders cowered in fear at the number of men arrayed against them, yet Avtandil was not afraid. He was no stranger to war. His heart held steady as he began issuing commands.

"Do not fear their might or number. Nothing can happen to us which is not ordained by God. However strong our allies or weak the foe, if this is the day of our deaths, we will perish. Yet, if our destiny prevails, I will slay all these evil men."

"The Knights who stand beside me know this, for it is our way. They are strong hearted like me, but you merchants have no skill or experience with battle. Lock yourselves safely away in the holds of our ship. Watch us from your place of safety and observe how we bring ruin to our enemy."

With the swiftness and grace of a panther, he put his armor on, still holding the wooden club. Then he moved to the prow of the ship, fearless in the face of the men bearing down on them. Wind from the waters blew his tattered and worn cape. To the merchants, he seemed to be an apparition, like the Shroud of Turin blowing on the breath of God. Then, Avtandil raised his club.

The pirates, fools to a man, counted the five warriors standing against their assault and cheered at the easy victory laid out before them. Fierce cries issued from mouths of golden teeth set in scarred and ugly faces. Their ship drew closer by the second, the iron shod beam of their ram ready to lay waste to the fragile merchant vessel.

Yet, the moment before it struck, Avtandil gave a deafening shout, swinging his club with both hands and every bit of strength he possessed. It connected just behind the head of the ram, splintering the wood, and sending the iron spinning down into the sea. The remains of the beam shattered into pieces when it struck Avtandil's ship. But he leaped over it, landing among the surprised pirates and drawing his sword.

Before they were able to react, he struck like a whirlwind, his steel blade cutting down man upon man. Soon the decks of the pirate vessel were slick with the blood of evil men, but he did not stop. Those who remained tried to rally against him, but their efforts were futile. Some were thrown into the deep by the ferocity of Avtandil's attacks, their armor drawing them down into a watery grave.

Others he hacked into bits, splitting the shields and skulls of some in a single blow, while those less fortunate were butchered limb by limb. From behind, his Knights joined the fray. Two of them engaged the pirates attempting to flank him. Meanwhile, the other two fired arrows into their enemies from afar. Within minutes, the will of their foe was broken.

Some men, knocked down by the might of Avtandil's blows, hid beneath corpses, stifling their fearful cries with bloodied hands. Others cowered and bleated like goats before the slaughter, begging in the name of God for mercy. Eight upon nine and nine upon eight were the men slain that day, as God has written. But as much as his heart desired the utter destruction of such evil, he stilled his hand and visited mercy upon them.

Those who begged forgiveness for their crimes and swore to serve were bound by oath and order. Despite their guilt, the freedom they craved would be earned through servitude and humility. Had they been educated, their penance may have been earned another way, but these were largely unenlightened men. They only understood how fear makes love and had not learned that vengeance alone belongs to God. Nor did they realize how forgiveness was a gift from Heaven into the hands of men.

The Arabian Knight gazed over the vessel as the recalcitrant pirates were tied. He took note of the ruined men left in the wake of his might. But he did not brag or boast. Those who speak of their greatness at such times are like drunkards who lack any courage save what they can salvage from the bottom of a cup. They forget how might and power are nothing without the Lord.

When the sun broke through the clouds, the truth of God's justice smiled on merchant ship and those aboard her. One could see clearly how those He protects have their enemies cut down equally, whether from a log or a sword. Through His grace, a tiny spark can burn down the greatest of trees, and the smallest of creatures can survive the worst fires. Knowing this, Avtandil was humble and kneeled, giving a silent prayer of thanks.

# CHAPTER 43 –

## WHAT LIES BENEATH

Seeing the battle had finished, Usam led the merchants out from hiding. They and the men of their caravan cheered the victory of their Knights. Their praises were near endless. A thousand tongues could not have given a greater measure of glory than they heaped about their heroes. Above all, they praised Avtandil.

Each came to him, kissing his head, face, hands, and feet. They bowed in servitude to the Arabian, maddened by the sight of his glory after the battle. He shone with some inner light, as if the hand of God rested on his brow and protected him.

"Lord in Heaven, thanks to You, the darkness of our night has broken, and daylight now shines down on us. We are saved by You and this Knight You have led to shepherd us against the world's evils. Truly, we are indebted to You and Your servant. Knowing this, we bind ourselves to him."

When Avtandil understood the merchants gave him praise in the same measure as God, he chastened them.

"What am I, other than a man of this earth? Your thanks belong to God alone, the Creator, and Maker of all. Only by His blessing do any of us stand here. We and the world were shaped and formed by His hands, as were the planets. Though they are not inanimate of spirit, they too are ordered around the sun by His decree. All men of wisdom follow their procession through the Heavens. But without Him, we are nothing. I am nothing."

"What have I done here, other than to slay the enemies of all that is good? From God, some things are revealed, and others hidden. He chose to spare your blood. Though I was His instrument, I must caution you against praising me for His work. He reveals some parts of this world, but not all. A wise man believes in what He on High has decreed instead of looking to the future."

"Now we have been given a gift. This pirate ship and the wealth of her hold rests in our hands. So do the souls of these men who have repented their evil ways. You may count what is here, though I will have no part of it, save what you may not seek to claim. You will know more of why later, but for now, let us see what manner and type of goods we have come to possess."

Then they went below decks, wary of hidden pirates but curious about what lay beneath. Soon, the glitter of gold shone back at them from the lanterns they held, and they understood just how much wealth the ship carried. It was full of stolen goods. Fine silks spilled out from crates and corners. Barrels of priceless wines were stacked high, resting in piles of more gold and gems than the traders had ever seen.

Bit by bit, they transferred the wealth of the pirate ship to their own vessel. It took more than a day to manage it all. When they finished, Avtandil ordered it sunk.

The men of the caravan broke holes in her sides, allowing water to slowly seep into the holds. They spread pitch over the wood, and every one of the merchants returned to their ship. From the top of their vessel, Avtandil lit and fired a single flaming arrow into the other ship's deck, setting the broken and battered vessel on fire.

Black smoke billowed into the sky as they watched her burn, and she sunk into the sea like a setting sun. It was a warning and a message. None but the Pirate King himself would disturb them further lest they meet a similar fate. As she sank beneath the waves, Usam turned to Avtandil and spoke.

"Your presence, through the grace of God, has strengthened us. We know our worth before you and find ourselves wanting. None among us is more than a candle to the light of your sun. Do not doubt that whatever we have is yours. Yet what you have given us in the form of this pirate treasure we now carry, can only be accepted on condition of our servitude to you. There are no other means by which we can repay your attention and kindness to our plight."

Avtandil, ever a Knight, took Usam's hands in his and held them high as he spoke.

"Who am I to ask even a single coin of you? At this moment, those who taste life have only God to thank. It is He who carried us through this. Without Him, my hands are no more than the thumbs of a blind man. Let us celebrate the joy you now keep about you, but please do not speak of gifts on my behalf."

"What do you imagine I might do with what you would give me? I have myself and my horse. However much treasure I might desire, it is already in my grasp, so I need nothing more. In Arabia, I am not a man of little means. But to you, my role now is as no more than a companion. We share a road together, though I will later have some dangerous business I must attend to."

"Take what you wish of the treasures we have liberated from these pirates. I will ask but one thing of you. This is the gift of your trust. I have something I wish to remain secret and will welcome your aid in achieving my desire."

"Until the time comes, do not speak of me as your master or a Knight. I will clothe myself as a merchant, like you. Tell all you meet that I am your chief. If you agree to keep this secret by the brotherhood between us, we have no debts. Together we will accomplish our goals, and in doing so, give glory to He on High."

The merchants rejoiced at his words, pleased they could be of service to him. They spoke of his face being like the sun. Each of them was thankful to bask in the glory of his presence. That night they sang many songs, making merry among themselves as their ship sailed ever east. Soon they would enter the Sea Realm, home of Melik Surkhavi, the fabled Sea King.

# CHAPTER 44 –

## THE CITY OF FLOWERS

Spiced winds from the distant eastern reaches of India blew them ever westward. They had been on the sea for nearly three weeks. The weather remained fair, though their heavily laden ship traveled slowly. In time, they spied land on the far horizon, and a joyous shout went up from the crew. All of them were tired of wind and water.

As they drew closer to the distant shores, they made out bright white buildings stretching down the coast as far as the eye could see. Ships and merchant vessels of all kinds and sorts dotted the waters. Tight formations of heavily armed Dromons sailed among them, flying the flag of the Sea King. The vigilance of Melik Surkhavi was not lost on Avtandil, though he said nothing of this to the men whose company he kept.

They entered the great port of the Sea Realm in a matter of hours. Towering statues of white marble stood on columns of gold to either side of the harbor entrance.

Men of war made their homes in fortresses lining the arms of the bay, where massive catapults stood ready to defend the city.

Horns blared across the waters, one note for ships entering and another for those departing. The merchants brought their ship into the line and were soon admitted. Guided by a small rowboat, they docked in the merchant quay and moored their ship with three large ropes.

Everyone on the ship marveled at the beauty of the city. They stared in awe at gardens and thickets of wondrous and rare flowers. The number and type of their color must have been drawn from every part of the rainbow, and they appeared draped over every corner and building. Only Heaven could compete with the perfume those blossoms spread through the air.

Soon inspectors came aboard to check their cargo against the manifest they presented. Porters were brought up the docks to offload goods, and Avtandil directed them, acting as the chief of Usam and his traders. He ordered their wares taken from here or there, accompanied by his men, bargaining, and bartering with sellers and buyers alike. After many hours of this, he noticed a gardener tending the flowers and called out to him.

"You there, I would know which port my ship has come to rest in. Whose man are you, and what of your King? Who is he, and how is this place called? More, tell me what is to be sold best here, for I would not cut my own hands through bad trading."

The man came forward, looking up at the Arabian with a mix of awe and surprise etched across his face. To him, it looked like lightning flashed from Avtandil's eyes, and his mouth was liquid ruby set with pearls. With reverence, he spoke to the Knight.

"I am Atikili Tenya, and I believe the sun which gives life to my flowers has left the gardens and been draped over you. In whatever way I might be of service, allow me. I assure you, no half-truths or lies will come to you from my lips. It is not within me to betray the sun from which these gardens take life. Since you are an incarnation of this light, I cannot speak falsely to you."

"These lands are the Sea Realm. They span a distance of five weeks travel by ship to the north and again to the south. Melik Surkhavi rules here, perfect and in fine health. He is the Sea King, and all here are subject to his rule. May God forever bless him."

"Where we stand is the fairest place in the entire Kingdom. It is known as Gulansharo, the city of flowers. I am chief among the gardeners, sworn to Usen, the Merchant King. In my gardens, you are as close to paradise as anyone may come until God embraces their soul and takes them to Heaven."

"Those who are old are rejuvenated by coming here. In summer and winter alike, we have flowers of every sort. Some for their beauty, and others we draw rare medicines from. All throughout the year, we are given to celebrating, drinking, and rejoicing at the wonder of our gardens. Even our enemies envy the beauty of this place. However, they cannot take it, for our walls are unassailable."

"From far and distant lands, merchants come to trade their wares. They buy and sell, gaining and losing as such men do. Their merchandise is gathered from all quarters. A poor trader can become wealthy in a month, and his servants will have money saved by the end of a year."

"Now, with your leave, let me tell you of my Lord Usen. This is his garden where you now rest, and it is he you must seek before any other. All traders who arrive speak to him first, lest the tithe and toll of their goods weigh too heavily upon them."

"What is best among your items, set aside to show the Merchant King. Let him choose to purchase what he wants from the fairest things before any other lays eyes on your wares. In doing this, Usen will free you to trade without impediment, so long as you are fair with the prices you ask of him. This is our custom, and you would be wise to respect it."

"But do not go to him yourself. When you are granted leave to show your wares, send one of your men. But first you must speak to his wife. Only through her can your man meet him. Her name is P'hatman Khathun, a Lady of her own worth. She is hospitable and kind. From her hand, many things are done, for she is equal in all ways to her husband, as it should be."

"It is our city's way for me to send someone to tell her when a merchant chief arrives. Yet, as you are the sun which gives life to my gardens, I beg your permission to inform her myself. With your blessing, I will tell her about you. She will send a man to meet you at daybreak."

Avtandil's listened to the man with surprise and happiness. His plans were working better than he expected. With a smile, he handed the man a rare and beautiful pearl. It was the same pale pink color as the coral roses hanging near them. With this gift, he permitted the man to do as he thought best. Joyously, the gardener ran off, eager to tell his Lady about the merchant chief.

He ran through the streets, weaving in and out of market stalls and dodging porters carrying goods, until coming to the palace of P'hatman. Still sweaty from his run, he went to the Lady, breathless with his news.

"My Lady, a young merchant chief has come. He has the face of a sun and eyes like lightning. Tall and lovely of form, he is like a well-grown cypress. With him are a host of merchants bearing priceless and exotic goods."

# CHAPTER 45 –

## MORE THAN A MERCHANT

When she received news of the stranger, Lady P'hatman listened with growing interest as the gardener spoke of how the young trader looked. She asked the man for more details, which he happily provided.

"How can I describe the youth? His skin is smooth like a moon of seven days. The folds of his coat rest about him like terraced gardens. For this, I came to you. What is your wish? May we send a man to invite this stranger here?"

P'hatman's face lit with curiosity as she heard about the merchant chief. She had sat too long in the absence of intrigue and wondered who the man might be or where he was from. Rather than waiting until morning to summon him, as was the custom, she sent ten servants and invited him to her apartments for dinner.

When Avtandil received his invitation, he was both surprised and pleased. His designs continued to work in his favor, which was a gift from God to him. As he readied himself, news of the unusual evening invitation spread throughout the merchant quarter.

Men and women alike came to watch as Avtandil made his way to the palace of Lady P'hatman. Those who saw him spoke in whispers of his rose-colored cheeks, seemingly cut of crystal and ruby. The jet and lightning of his eyes seared those who gazed on him. They compared the power of his arms to a lion. Some seven aid the grace of his stride was like a panther.

Many who looked on him were carried away with desire, bereft of their hearts. The souls of housewives grew weary, and husbands were left empty of spirit. As one, they wanted no more than to gaze on the Arabian until nightfall. But he would not be delayed and did not stray from his course.

P'hatman, the wife of the Merchant King Usen, met Avtandil at the door to her palace. She was curious to see if the rumors of this foreigner were true, and he did not disappoint her. The sight of him stole the breath from her breast. Never had she seen a man like him.

Yet she was also beautiful, and not one to burden the eye. Though not young, she was the picture of elegance and grace. A woman of her own right, subservient to none. Her form was lithe and graceful, crowned by a lovely face.

Dark hair wound its way down her back in long braids, with here and there an emerald or sapphire shining back. Her skin color was like dark coffee mixed with a twist of delicate cream and a pinch of sugar. Of her lips, they could only be compared to ripe plums, soft and sweet, begging for the nectar of affection.

The two of them, Knight, and Lady, stared at one another. Though distance separated each, the energy and magnetism between them sent sparks throughout the room. They saluted one another, he on one knee, and she, bowing in honor towards the gentleman before her.

Their greeting was not long, though it seemed like an

eternity to them. Each of their hearts reached across the distance separating them yet stopped short. It seemed they were afraid to collide for fear of the avalanche of emotion it might unleash. But those watching understood nothing of this. For secrets shared between the eyes of the worthy are more hidden than the gateway to Heaven.

Their meeting passed in little more than a moment, and then P'hatman invited him in. They went up the stairs of her palace to the dining room and seated themselves. Soon food and drink arrived, and Avtandil began to understand the depth and complexity of the woman before him.

She adored fine and rare things, which became more apparent as the night passed. Music and wine graced the evening. Many a lovely lady entertained them, singing with the voices of angels. The food they ate was crafted with care and attention by the finest chefs in Gulansharo. Meanwhile, they presented gifts to one another, drinking and eating as those around them spoke with joy as to the occasion of their meeting.

The two of them stayed late into the evening, enjoying themselves until their meal and more than a few bottles of wine were done. Satisfied, the Knight had no room in his heart for want of more, save perhaps companionship. With the pale moon high in the Heavens, they parted ways. Avtandil returned to his ship and rested. His soul at peace for the first time in many years, for he imagined a glimmer of hope in their meeting.

In the morning, he had his men show their wares to the merchant Lords of Usen. They selected the best items for the King, as agreed, and counted out the payment. From there, Avtandil and the members of his caravan were given leave to trade as they wished. Only those among his crew knew he wasn't a trader, but they kept their word, selling and bartering, but never revealing the Knight's identity.

Meanwhile, P'hatman called on him with increasing frequency. Many were the days they could be found sitting together late into the night or walking in the gardens. Before long, the fires of love began to lick at her.

The depth and sincerity of their conversations drew her in, and she became like Vis, lost without Ramin. And for his own heart, Avtandil was not immune to what grew between them, yet he kept himself apart. He had other designs and refused to let desire distract him.

Not being a fool, he knew if a man was strong enough to remain aloof from a woman, he would do better for himself. For women often play with and please the hearts of men, winning their faith and trust. Yet they cut and pierce the strong and weak with equal measure. This, he knew, was the reason a strong man should keep his secrets and heart close when dealing with a woman, particularly one so lovely and enchanting as P'hatman.

Those who are both wise and strong, as Avtandil was, know the extent of a woman's heart. A man wants what he wants, and a woman holds her own passions. But all is lost should a man voice his feelings before desire. It shows the weakness of his heart, and women do not respect weak men any more than men respect wantonness in a woman.

Yet, though P'hatman was a woman with her vices, she was also a Lady. It pained her to keep secret the desire she felt for Avtandil, but she said nothing. At least, not at first. But with time, the affection she had for him grew until it became difficult for her to control.

# CHAPTER 46 –

## THE FLOWER OF GULANSHARO

Soon, the seed planted by love sprouted, and with each day, it found new heights. Before long, she could not conceal her longing for him or hide her woe at his absence. Tears fell from her eyes as she lamented her plight, seeking a solution but sure of no road. She wanted what her heart desired.

"What must I do, and what will become of me? I am torn by my love for this man. I feel no different than a rose forced to choose between the intimate caress of a nightingale and the light of the sun. He will lose all respect for me if I tell him about the desires consuming my heart. Then, even the sight of him will become rare to me."

"Yet, if I say nothing, I will perish in the flames of love. I can think of no way I might bind him to me. Nor can I see how to save myself from this pain. So, what does it matter in the end if I speak or say nothing?"

"I will tell him of my heart and live or die by his

decision. Let one fate or the other belong to me, for no one ever found safety in the middle of a road. And anyway, what ailment can a physician cure when the patient does not reveal the truth of their hurt? But how will I say this to him? I think it must be done with discretion, lest he take offense, so I will write to him."

Then P'hatman put pen to paper and began to draft a letter to Avtandil. She would tell him of her love and desire for him, but not in any passing manner. The words she chose would be precise, composed from poetry and elegance. She would reveal her suffering and hunger for him with each stroke and line.

Perhaps his heart would be moved. Such writing is not easily put aside except by the ignorant or simple-minded. She knew Avtandil was a man who stood tall among other men. He was the embodiment of truth, given shape and form by the hand of God. With the Lord's blessing, her words would reach his heart, and perhaps she would achieve her desire.

"I hope it is not your wish to bring woe upon those who are too long separated from you. Yet nearness to you has consumed me with fire. Though it is a joy to see your face, you shine too brightly. It appears God created you like a sun, and I fear it is my plight to have been burned by being too near your rays. In your presence, I cannot find words."

"My breath becomes shortened when I am close to you, as though the shadow of my days grows longer. I am sure those who gaze on the fullness of your form can do no more than devote themselves to you. For me, your glance is sweeter than honey. It begs the attention of my caresses, and I want no more than to unite them with you."

"To my eyes, your visage is undeniable. I wonder at the rose of your form. How does it not cause the nightingale to quiver and shake with ecstasy at the thought of being near you? Perhaps I too could plead for your time, but to what end? Words will still fail me, and fainting would only earn me pity."

"God as my witness, your beauty withers the flowers of Gulansharo, and my own beauty fades with them. The beams of your sun scorch me. I would beg to entertain you in private under the pale moonlight. Otherwise, your fire might consume me. Unable to control myself, I would surely perish in its intensity."

"Yet, I find myself luckless in this, for what can I do? Patience departs me. I am maddened for want of your gaze. The black of your lashes strikes me anew each morning with the firmness and force of a lash. Though I beg for the pleasure it brings, if I possessed the means to end my suffering, I would avail myself of it. But there is no road left to me. You are my one hope. I beg Heaven to lengthen the day so I might see more of you."

"In your absence, life has become a thing I endure rather than enjoy. However much I pray to hasten the time when I will know your decision, the hurt in my heart does not lessen. I wait like a flower in the rain, unable to realize my own fate and begging the return of her sun."

"If there is any way you can help me, I will forever be your servant. For, without your aid, my wits are lost. My mind and body grow wild while my spirit and heart falter. With this letter, I seek an answer from you. Until that time, I will not know whether your words and strong hands will slay me or undress these chains about my body and set me free."

With a final pen stroke and a dash of perfume, she signed her name and finished the letter. Though tears stained the pages and caused the ink to bleed through in places, she did not care. Her heart was on her sleeve, and she had no choice but to give voice to it or perish in the attempt. Light and life had become nothing to her without him only he could provide her with an answer.

She summoned her two most trusted servants. Their skin was black as pitch, for they were of the Kadj race, but the two had long since been cast out from the empire of Kadjeti. No other royal houses in Gulansharo would give them shelter, but P'hatman had taken them in. She had given them new purpose, and their allegiance to her was surer than the sun rising in the east and setting in the west. It was to them she entrusted her secret and its delivery.

# CHAPTER 47 –

## THE SORCERER'S MESSAGE

Avtandil stood on the balcony of his apartments, staring into the eastern sea, and enjoying the beauty of Gulansharo. His mind wandered to Tariel. He wondered how his friend fared or if Asmath had been able to mend his wounds. But his thoughts were interrupted by a soft step behind him.

He whirled around, reaching for his dagger, but the hand of another was already on it. Surprised, he looked up to see the smiling faces of two men he remembered as servants of P'hatman. Their wide white grins shone at him from black faces, and they bowed before speaking.

"Good sir, our intent is neither to harm you nor to disturb your thoughts. However, our mistress, Lady P'hatman, ordered us to present you with this letter from her hand. She wished the contents and delivery to remain secret for all but you. Thus, we have come as we did, with a touch of our Kadj sorcery. As the letter is now in your hands, we will take our leave."

Avtandil hardly blinked, and the two men were gone again. One moment they were in front of him, and the next, no more. It was as if the wind blew them away like smoke from a shuttered candle flame. He could not say how they came or where they had gone. None could, he supposed, for what it meant to be Kadj was a mystery to all. But at that moment, P'hatman's letter was of more interest to him than the riddles of sorcery.

With curious hands, he broke the wax seal of her letter and untied the red ribbon holding the parchment closed. As he unrolled the paper, the scent of her perfume wafted up from it. He remembered her as his eyes scanned the words she gifted him, though his thoughts were not entirely kind.

"Who is this woman to send sorcerers to my doorstep with words such as these? While I am not blind to her beauty or charms, she does not know how my heart belongs to another. Tinatin is the woman I desire, and she is as different from P'hatman as the day is from night."

"How can I compare the beauty of my love with that of Lady P'hatman? One is a bright and innocent sun of blue skies and faith, while the other is a dark and smoky night of incense and temptation. I cannot deny the beauty of either of them, for I am a man. But no commonality exists between these two women."

"Tinatin is a sweet nightingale, and P'hatman is a wise raven. But what do ravens have to do with roses? Yet, she does not ask me to attend to her in brevity, so perhaps her words carry some weight. For unfitting deeds are brief and thus bear no fruit. So, what is the point or purpose in them for one who is true of heart?"

"If I can find no justice in this letter, I fear my hands are bound. My heart has willingly been given to the aid of Tariel, and for his sake, I seek Nestan. News of her by any means is of inestimable value to me. Therefore, I must do everything in my power for her and for the sake of my friend. To do anything less would be unbecoming, no matter what I may prefer for myself."

"With this letter, P'hatman has planted a seed. I cannot ignore the heat growing in me from what she wrote, for she is a desirable woman. Neither can I forget how much I need her help. Without her aid, I will remain a wanderer. My lot will be like that of an untethered ship, drifting to and from, with no port or home to call my own."

"Of all the citizens in Gulansharo, her home is the most open. She entertains countless merchants and visitors from all quarters and keeps sorcerers as servants. I am certain information flows through her court like souls crossing the river Styx. If any know what I seek, she will be the one. And if she does not know, perhaps no one knows of Nestan or her fate."

"I did not plan this route, but I dare not say I have no desire for P'hatman. She is undeniably lovely, and however much I may want another solution, I am not blind nor so old as to make a diet of milk and rice. Though many roads may lead towards a man's destination, only one will lead him home."

"If she loves me and we are intimate, her heart will be mine. She will not count the weight of shame or dishonor. Her every secret will be open, and whatever she is aware of will be shared with me. For this reason alone, I must consent to her wishes. Perhaps therein I may find the answers I seek."

He thought long on what he must say and how to say it. Becoming intimate with P'hatman was far from his first wish, yet the thought was not an ugly thing to him. She was a woman, refined and shapely. More, her mind and wit were sharp. His consideration of these things was not without passion, though his intent and wish had never been to betray the trust of Tinatin.

"If the planets do not favor a course, how might a man make his way? I do not have what I want, and I do not want what I have. This twilight leaves me wandering in a haze. Yet, it seems the city of Gulansharo is where I will learn how to pay my debts, for whatever rests within a pitcher, the same will flow out. Let us find out what comes from spending our passions together."

His course of action decided, Avtandil took up his own pen, dipping the end into the ink well and setting himself to composing a letter. Knowing the fickle nature of desire in a woman, he kept his answer short and direct. In this way, he hoped to further fan the flames that burned her, making her more compliant to his will.

# CHAPTER 48 –

## WHEN HUNTER BECOMES HUNTED

"**I** have received your letter and welcome your praise. Though I must say, you are not the only one who suffers from the fires of passion. Love burns me too, and my heart lightens to know you have anticipated me. As it is your wish and mine, I would enjoy your company without delay or interruption. Let us swim the sea of our longing, and bathe in the arms of one another."

The letter finished, he sealed it, pressing the mark of his ring into the soft wax before it cooled. Then he summoned one of the Knights Phridon had sent with him. The man was instructed to deliver his message directly into the hands of Lady P'hatman.

To say she received his letter with joy would be to compare the sun to a candle. Her breath grew heavy as she read what he wrote, and her heart began to beat with renewed intensity. She could barely keep her pen on the paper as she wrote her reply.

"Absent the grace and beauty of your form, I see the

tears I have shed are sufficient. Tonight, come to me. I will be alone and waiting to receive you in my arms and elsewhere. When twilight kisses the edges of the sky, my lips too shall be waiting for yours."

As before, the two Kadj sorcerers delivered her message to Avtandil. He read it with surprise. Her invitation and declaration she sent were more direct than anything he had ever seen a woman write. The boldness of her request turned the flames of his desire into a raging furnace.

Passion rose unbidden in him, breaking free from his control and threatening to drown him. At once the hunter became the hunted. All he could think of were the shapes of her curves beneath his hands. Tonight, he would have her. Nothing and no one would stand in his way.

Taking note of the sun crossing the sky's edge, he judged there were two hours left until twilight. During that time, he bathed himself, commanding fine clothes to wear from the merchants' stocks, and tidied himself up. It would not do well for him to appear before Lady P'hatman in any form other than his best.

When ready, he left his apartments and casually made his way towards her palace. Twilight crept towards the sky from the east, like fog over a river in the morning. Soon all Gulansharo was blanketed in shadow, and one of the Kadj sorcerers stepped out of the darkness, stopping Avtandil with a warning hand. He said an urgent matter had presented itself and the Lady could not see him this evening. She was unavailable, and he must turn back.

Frustrated at the delay and the overwhelming press of his unfulfilled desire, he pushed past the sorcerer. He would no more be delayed than the moon, which would soon be in the night sky. Unspent passion raged inside of him, blinding his judgment. Who was this woman to turn him away at the last moment? One does not invite a lion to dinner and leave him on the porch like a cat.

Without hesitation, he made his way to her palace with bold and sure strides. The doormen, uninformed as to the change of heart their Lady had, welcomed him in, and he made his way towards her rooms. He took the stairs one at a time, each one lighting anew the fires of desire raging in him.

By the time he reached her chambers, blood was coursing through his veins. His whole body ached, and he pushed open the doors without knocking or announcing himself. She stood when he came in, looking up at him and timid beneath the intensity of his gaze. Something troubled her, but she did not speak of it, and he did not address it. She promised herself to him this night, and she would be his. He would not be denied.

Crossing the room, he took her into his arms and pressed his lips to hers. For a moment, she hesitated, but her own desire mirrored his power, and she could not restrain herself. She wrapped herself around him, putting a hand behind his head and pulling him into her embrace.

They fell upon one another, and the world faded around them as the intensity of their passion bathed the room. Neither thought of anything other than melting into the other. They pushed back and forth, exploring one another. Lips brushing ears and cheeks as they whispered heated words. In those moments, there was no other person anywhere in the word for either of them.

Soon, the questions which lay unanswered between them were forgotten. Their passions mingled until, at last, there was only one voice between them. It sang a melody older than time, moving with the same rhythm which birthed the universe.

Their power spent, they lay together in a heap of arms and legs. Sweat covered their bodies, yet each still longed for the closeness of the other. So, they did not move or try to rise. Instead, they stared into one another's eyes, the waters of rising once more between them as the flames of desire rekindled their passion.

But there was a crash from the hall, and then the door burst open. The lovers were interrupted by an elegant and graceful youth. He stood in the doorway, looking at them. Behind him, his manservant stood with a sword and shield at the ready.

P'hatman clung to Avtandil in terror, trembling at the sight of the stranger and his man-at-arms. The youth stepped in, gazing in wonder and surprise at the two lovers. He looked over them both before speaking to her.

"I think the road before me has become rocky. But do not allow me to interrupt your evening. I will not hinder you but know this much you evil woman. You have shamed me with your wickedness, and I will cause you to regret your time with this man when day breaks."

"Tomorrow, you will receive what payment awaits you for the ill you have visited upon me. I will make you suffer as no woman has before. Mark my words woman, I will see you eat your own children one bite at a time. Spit on my beard and let me run through the fields like a madman if I fail to do this!"

Then, the man leaned toward them, touching his beard as he did so. This was an invitation to insult him if he failed to do as he said. With this gesture, he clarified the intent and certainty of his promise to ruin the Lady.

Looking at the two of them once more, he spit on the floor before turning and leaving, forcefully slamming the door shut as he left. The sound echoed across the room with the finality of a coffin slamming closed. It was an audible affirmation of the inevitable doom awaiting Lady P'hatman and her children when the sun rose.

# CHAPTER 49 –

# THE WAY FORWARD

Life hangs forever in the balance, and silence often measures the heartbeats of those doomed to die. Not even a second passed between the door slamming and the reaction of those within. Yet, like words unwritten in a poem, the empty spaces hung in the air much longer.

In an instant, things which could have been and were not stood out in stark contrast to what was. The moment might have lasted forever, were it not shattered by a cry. With a long wailing sob, P'hatman began beating her head. She screamed and scratched at her cheeks as she did so.

Choking on her tears, she shuddered in Avtandil's arms. Though she tried to speak, her words were lost to a sadness he did not know anything about. As he held her crumpled form, what she said slowly became more understandable, and he finally heard what she said.

"Bring out the women of the wall, those who have lost

their men to the sea or worse. Let them cast stones upon me and break my head until all I am is mingled with the earth. I have killed my children and slain my husband!"

"My shameful actions have made an end of me. I will be forever separated from my darlings. All we own has been given by me as loot. Because of me, nothing good will come to those I have loved and cherished in this life!"

Avtandil was confused. The woman who had just passionately rocked her body against his moments ago was now shipwrecked on the shores of a tragedy he knew nothing of. She was a temptest of emotion, broken and battered by some invisible storm. Concerned for her well-being and state of mind, he asked her to explain.

"Woman, I cannot understand what pains you so. Tell me why you lament the appearance of this youth as though he were the reaper of souls. What does he want, and why did he make such dark threats to you and your children? What fault has he found in you?"

When P'hatman heard his words, she stopped bemoaning the hand Fate had dealt her. She looked at him with a steady gaze. Although tears still streamed from her eyes, she took his hands in hers before speaking.

"Can you not see how I am mad with tears and grief? Do not ask me of him or what he desires. There is no time now for my tongue to explain such things. My own hand has brought an end to the children I love most in this world. How can I find joy or peace in the ruin of my life?"

"I allowed my impatience for your love to lay waste to all I hold dear. Composure fled my side, and with it what good judgment I had. If I were one to utter idle words or a street gossip who is unable to keep secrets, then so be it!"

"But I am not mad or witless. I do not roam the streets, raving to all who pass to help me with their lamentations. Surely you realize I am sane. Yet I have hurt myself. It is my hand which caused this wound. No physician can heal someone who drinks their own blood."

"Now you are caught by him too, though it was not by my choice. I told you to stay away this evening, but when I saw you... When your arms were around me... I had no power or wish to stop myself, and now all is lost. You are also at risk, though you do not understand why yet."

"Now, only two ways forward are open to you. Choose whichever of them you wish, but do not waste yourself on me out of desire. For with one choice, there may be nothing left of us both. Yet, I will surely be destroyed by the other. Put your longings and hopes to rest and make your decision quickly, for time is of the essence."

"First, if you are able, go and kill that man. Slay him in secret tonight. You will save me and all I hold dear from the wrath of his vengeance if you do this. I will not be forced to eat my own children, and the people of my house will not be slaughtered. If you do this, I will tell you the reason for my tears."

"Yet, if you prefer another course of action, I understand. I do not want to see you brought to the same end as me. In this case, gather everything you need for your journey, and escape from Gulansharo tonight with your men. Should you stay, the man you saw will bring me before the court, and my sins will become your own."

Avtandil restrained the urge declare himself a Knight of Arabia. Instead, he was mindful of his disguise as a wealthy merchant. The deed P'hatman asked of him was an opportunity to absolutely bind her to his will and learn whatever he desired. Although he did not know who the man was or his grievance against her, it did not matter. Taking her hands in his, he promised to aid her.

"My Lady, it would be remiss of me to ignore the threats this man has made against you and your children. It is true, I am no warrior, but I dare not call myself any sort of man and in the same breath abandon you to the evil he has spoken. Although you called this man a Knight, I cannot think of him as an equal, let alone as a threat."

"Such men are often less than the servants who call them Lord. So, give me one of your Kadj sorcerers as a guide. Let him accompany me and show me the way. He will witness the events of this night. You will have the truth of what happens and whether I succeed or perish. Aside from this, you must wait and be patient. With God's grace, I may prevail against him."

P'hatman knelt before him and cried as he spoke. She was worried about herself and her children but also for his safety. His skill as a warrior was yet unknown to her. Her heart feared she sent a bold youth into the den of a lion. Little did she realize it was a lion she was sending to visit a bold youth. Yet, she had no one else to save her or help carry her burdens.

"His name is Kuru Shifta. He is a skilled Knight and an exceedingly cruel man, as you witnessed from his speech. These days he is the wine taster for our King, but some say the man used to be a bandit. I do not know if those rumors are true. All I can tell you is that he never sleeps alone. There are always men at his door and likely more in his chambers guarding him."

"I will do as you ask and send one of my sorcerers as a guide and a witness. He will show you the way and perhaps may be of some little assistance. If by some miracle you can slay Kuru, I beg of you, take my ring from him. He stole it from me some time ago and wears it as a reminder of things I cannot tell you now. You will find it on the small finger of his left hand."

# CHAPTER 50 –

## BURDENS OF THE PAST

When P'hatman finished speaking, she touched a trinket around her neck. No sooner had she done so than both of her Kadj sorcerers appeared at the door. She ordered one to remain with her and sent the other to guide the Arabian.

She believed her lover went to meet his doom, but she had no other choice. And, for his part, Avtandil did not hesitate. He was eager to go and took a heavy iron mace in his hands as left her chambers. Tonight, blood would be spilled.

Together, Knight and sorcerer passed through the city. They went like ghosts, slipping from shadow to shadow. All eyes appeared to turn away from them, and their steps made no more sound than a cat on the prowl. Before long, they arrived at the upper reaches of a palace cut into the cliffs overlooking the sea.

It was made of green and red bloodstone and sat atop a

series of terraced buildings and gardens. A lone room rested at its highest point, facing the water. From where Avtandil sat, he could see a door, and the edges of a single balcony. Two men stood guard at the entrance, occasionally pacing back and forth. This was where the sorcerer pointed as he described it.

"The building you see is formed of solid walls, with only one entrance. Therein, you will find Kuru. The man has a black heart and many enemies. I cannot tell you if he is awake or asleep, but I am certain more than the two men you see guard his slumber."

"I must warn you to be cautious and quiet. Should you raise any alarm, men will swarm over you like ants upon a rotting corpse. You will meet a gruesome end, which I would not want to report back to my Lady."

Avtandil nodded his understanding and thanked the sorcerer. With stealth and caution, he slowly crept toward the place where his enemy slept. He kept to the shadows as he went, careful to remain hidden until finally reaching the entrance of the small palace. There, he stealthily crept towards the two guards standing watch.

He waited until one turned away and reached a hand up over the mouth of the man closest to him. Then he opened the unfortunate soul's throat with a single motion, spraying blood through the air. Before the second guard could react or cry out, Avtandil smashed the head of the man he had just killed into the face of the one who still lived.

With a sickening crack, the heads of the two guards collided like ripe gourds. Brains and hair mingled like clay and straw, and the two corpses crumpled in a bloody heap. Making sure no one had seen him, he carefully lifted the bar on the door, and silently let himself into the room.

The man he had come for was sleeping on a bed of fine silks. His left hand rested across his chest, with

P'hatman's jeweled ring glittering from his smallest finger. Another guard stood watch at the entrance to the balcony, but Avtandil easily dispatched him with a single blow from the heavy iron mace he held. Now he was free to work.

Still bloodied from the ruin he visited on the outer door guards, he reached down and grabbed Kuru by the face and head. Lifting the startled man into the air, he slammed him to the ground and stabbed a knife through his heart. Though the man struggled fiercely, Avtandil held him down until the weight of the afterlife dimmed the light in his eyes, and he became as still as the night.

Then he cut the small finger from Kuru's lifeless hand, ensuring P'hatman's ring was still on it. Satisfied with his efforts, he threw the corpses from the balcony and down to the water's edge. Their bodies were dashed to pieces on the rocks below, leaving a ruined mess of men who would forever be bereft of tomb. Before morning, the tide would drag their remains away to feed the crabs. No spade would find a grave for them, nor mourners lament their passing.

Such was the fire and fury of the Arabian lion. Those who gazed on him in admiration faced a warm sun. But whoever was foolish enough to stand against him met the terror and fury of his wrath. Without wiping his bloodied knife, Avtandil turned and left.

He returned to the sorcerer, who smiled at his success. No one heard any sound from the slaughter he visited on Kuru and his men. His work done, they returned to the palace of P'hatman, once more moving through the streets like shadows and smoke.

When they were back at P'hatman's palace, they went directly to her chambers. Without care for decorum or cleaning the bloodstains from himself, Avtandil came in and announced the completion of his task.

"The sun of Kuru's life has set forever. No more will

he disturb you or threaten your family. Here is the small finger from his left hand, with your ring still upon it. And of myself and my knife, you need not ask for evidence. Surely the blood covering me speaks for itself."

"Now, tell me why this man spoke to you as he did. What was it he held over you? How does his death set your children free and release you from the cage of his cruelty? I would know now, for blood is on my hands tonight, and a fire still burns in my heart."

P'hatman did not speak at first. She was horrified at the sight of Kuru's severed finger and shocked by the presence of so much blood. Yet she was unable to contain her relief at being released from whatever threats the slain man had once kept her captive with. She fell to her knees, embracing Avtandil's legs, and praised him.

"Where in the world could I have found a Hero such as you? I am not worthy of looking at your face, nor to be here beneath your gaze. You have healed my wounded heart, and now I may extinguish the fires which before ruined me. My husband Usen and our children are born anew by your hand."

"You are a lion and without equal. I do not know how we might magnify our praise of you, but I will give what you ask. Your hand has spilled blood on my account, and mine must now deliver what was promised."

"Sit, bloodied as you are, and I will tell you the tale. Though it may take all night to finish, I would ask you to stay here with me these next few days. I cannot be alone with the burden of what has passed, nor with the knowledge of what I asked you to do on my behalf."

"Now, seat yourself, and prepare to listen..."

# CONTINUING THE JOURNEY –

## DIFFICULTY AT THE BEGINNING

Lost in my thoughts, I failed to notice the music die or the dancers leave the stage. Instead, I woke in a daze, like a man coming up from the water. The dream of Nino's performance still colored everything I saw. Red stage lights left my hands looking as if they were wet with the blood of P'hatman's lover.

I clutched my journal to my chest as though protecting the children of her and Usen. My eyes were still not adjusted to the world around me, and I needed time to cleanse them of the beauty and tragedy which stained my sight. Avtandil had done things I could not have imagined, but I understood the course he chose.

Moreover, I was strangely enchanted by the idea of a woman like P'hatman. She was refined and raw, but so much more than I felt I truly grasped. My own desire stirred within me at thoughts of a lady so rare as her. A gem refined by the complexities and deceptions of life.

Her plight and the resultant deaths it caused made me wonder about how we define ourselves as human. We evaluate and measure others by standards we're often loathe to be judged by. Then we listen to the voices of our great leaders, despite the fact of their truths almost always being well dressed lies.

Too often, it was impossible to separate fact from fiction. The ignorant knew better than the enlightened, and stupidity seemed to eternally rule over intelligence. I seemed to have made the same mistakes in chasing the story I so desperately sought, for it appeared to have taken a similar turn.

I had lost the thread of it, and too late realized the folly of my actions. Like a fox chasing a rabbit down a hole, I expected to find a meal in the form of an enchanting poem or sweet parable. Instead, this Georgian epic washed the myriad emotions of life, love, and death over me.

Now the pages were bloodied, and I was unable to remove the narrative from my heart. The poetry consumed my mind. I was forced to ask myself if I was nothing more than an arrogant foreigner, taking notes on something I didn't understand. Or had the story begun showing me how to be something more?

Was I more like Avtandil or the youth he killed? I wondered who the young man might have been and what he had done so wrong. We all make mistakes. In fact, if it weren't for some mistakes, most of us wouldn't be here. So why did he have to die?

I couldn't find any redemption in his death, but his story was out of pages. There was nothing left to write of him, save perhaps a eulogy for the tragedy of life unspent. But then, aren't we all a little like him sometimes? Too aware of our strengths, but blind to the trap of our own inadequacies.

All these thoughts and more raced through my mind as

I sat there. I didn't realize how long or far I'd wandered into my head until the usher came and asked why I was sitting alone in the theater. When I stared up at the man, he gazed down at my tear-streaked face like a father and asked how he could help me.

Instinctively trusting him, I explained all my experiences in Georgia. I told him of the story I so desperately sought. When I finished, he smiled and spoke with soft tones in answer to my question.

"Every Georgian knows this story by heart, but you are a foreigner. You do not know that God has given man no language other than our own tongue which can truly show you the beauty of this tale. Yet, some of us believe our poem has been kept a secret from the world for too long."

"Perhaps we have hidden our treasure too well, and this caution has caused some of our people to lose sight of the deeper meanings. My advice is to continue your search. Look hard enough and you will see the end. If you're lucky, you might also find something more important."

"I'm sure you know how every story has an end, but to understand how a thing happened, you need to look beyond the ending. To do this, you must return to the beginning. For no tree falls before it has been a seed. But every seed is aware of its history, just as every dance carries the steps of those who came before."

"But the truth is, we all dance. The earth is forever spinning. One has but to take a step to begin dancing. Every child instinctively understands this, but as they grow, the noise of living drowns out the music of life. Few of them ever find it again. In time age and experience cause them to forget they once knew how to dance. The next time they shine is also their last, for it is the moment they leave this earth and see the lights of Heaven."

"Tonight, you have seen Nino, who glows like a sun, but it is not within my power to show her to you again.

Her star shines elsewhere now, and she is gone. But if you come here tomorrow evening, I will share a secret with you."

"Be here exactly when the full moon rests over this theater. If you possess the courage, you may find what you seek. Follow your heart, and maybe you'll have a chance to see where your own story starts. Or, at least as much of it as any man or woman has an ability to understand..."

# THANK YOU!

We hope you enjoyed The Road to Gulansharo.
Make sure to read all three books in the series.

**Avtandil's Quest**
**The Road to Gulansharo**
**A Rule of Three**

If you'd like to learn more about us,
please visit our website or follow us online!

## https://hjbuell.com

@HJBUELL

# ABOUT THE AUTHORS

## H. J. BUELL

Henry is a native of Virginia who grew up between the majesty of the Blue Ridge Mountains and the secret societies of Washington, D. C. Over time his profession drew him into the wars of Afghanistan, Iraq, and the complexities of geopolitics. But one day, he left the war.

From there he traveled the old world on foot, staying in different countries, while learning their beliefs, cultures, and customs until reaching Georgia. While working as a lecturer and writer, a publisher introduced him to Shota Rustaveli's epic poem, The Knight in the Panther Skin.

The story captured his imagination, and he began working to translate the poem's esoteric, philosophical, and spiritual elements into English. However, it took seven years to accurately rewrite the epic.

And now, the complete series can be read in English for the first time in history. These books are Avtandil's Quest, The Road to Gulansharo, and A Rule of Three, and they are available in eBook and print, either online or from select bookstores.

# ABOUT THE AUTHORS

## ANA GABUNIA

A native of the old Georgian city of Kutaisi, Ana lived through the darkest times of modern Georgia. As a child, she studied French by candlelight and dreamt of making the world a better place. It was there, on her father's lap by the flickering light of a single flame, where she first discovered The Knight in the Panther Skin. He read the legend to her, and this ancient tale imprinted itself on her heart forever.

In time she grew from a little girl into a woman full of hopes and dreams. She studied diplomacy and journalism, working with the United Nations, where she tirelessly championed the rights of internationally displaced people, women, and children. Before long she worked her way into the Georgian Diplomatic reserves.

Eventually she traveled across Europe, yet the truths she hoped to find abroad weren't there. Instead, they were back home in Kutaisi, where her love for the beauty and philosophy of The Knight in the Panther Skin first blossomed. Realizing how few people knew the story outside of Georgia, she committed herself to bringing this epic tale to the world.